Tame The Mind

An Exploration of

Love | Sex |Happiness

A Novel by

Asha Menon, MD

Published by Life Lessons LLC 2020

Cover software and designs by The Longtail Ad.

Email: tamethemind360@gmail.com

Website: https://tamethemind.org

Names: Menon, Asha, Author

Title: Tame The Mind

An exploration of Love, Sex, Happiness

Identifiers: ISBN: e-book 978-1-7334486-0-4

ISBN: Paperback 978-1-7334486-1-1

Library of Congress Control Number: 2020905966

Subjects:Romance/MentalHealth/Spirituality/Relationship/Self-help.

Published in the United States of America by Life Lessons LLC.

All the characters in this book are fictitious. Any resemblance to the living or dead is coincidental and unintentional.

PRAISES FOR TAME THE MIND: AN EXPLORATION OF LOVE, SEX, HAPPINESS.

"In *Tame the Mind*, Asha Menon writes on **the 'age-old' issues that society too often chooses to sweep under the rug: sexuality, marital dissatisfaction, female desire.** Tied to the challenges of the immigrant experience, Ms. Menon presents an exploration of the many hues of modern life. I wish her all the best in her writing and her future endeavors."--**Dr. Shashi Tharoor, Member of Parliament and author of more than 17 books.**

" Be prepared for some self-assessment. I highly recommend this book to everyone. It really makes you think about life. Things aren't always as they seem. **It will give you a whole new outlook on life**." Kim Vandevalk, CA.

"Well written first novel. **High in readability**. Easy to relate to characters. **Suffused with practical psychology and philosophy. Dares to take on big themes of love, sex, and loss. Highly recommended**!" Dr. Abby Kurien, Psychiatrist, NJ.

"It is not a one-time read. **It is a keeper,** and it will find a **place in my collection! Colorful characters, a nice plot, and sub-plots** that keep you **engrossed**. Some nice homilies also in the form of diary entries of one of the characters.**!"** Nanda Nayar.

"**A very well-written book touching the taboos of extramarital life, strained relations, being at peace, and setting oneself free**. A theme many have inhibitions to write. Felt like falling out of love is more powerful than falling in love. And the **author did not try to hide any stark realities** we all face in our lives. A very good self-assessment book. **Worth reading** !!!" Ajith Hariharan IT Entrepreneur.

"**Easy, Quick Read with Great Insights**. This book was **a great short read on a meaningful topic. I could not put the book down because it was highly engaging each step of the way. The character development and story unfold beautifully, and I highly recommend** anyone even remotely interested in this book purchase it IMMEDIATELY! You won't regret it!" Upkar Grewal.

"**This book is a bible for relationships.** Everyone who is in any kind of relationship should read this book because, for most of them, it will be an **eye-opener** on how to deal with the problems we are facing every day." Ania.

"**Entertaining ... movie material. The characters are riveting**. One can **visualize every scene. Flows well**. The portrayal of human emotions and dialogues is impressive." Dr. Rama Reddy.

"**This book was my second book in this genre, first being 'The Notebook' 'Tame The Mind' was intriguing, and I finished it in one sitting.** Tame The Mind covers life from a woman's view, like the need for physical and emotional companionship, sex, marital inequality, death (this part was very touching), and a brief encounter with office politics. **The quotes and poetry were fabulous. I might run through them again, for they were insightful. I would love to read more books from the author**." Gopal, Senior Executive.

"**Was hooked** after the first chapter and **could not put the book down. Brilliant. The language is impressive.** Enjoyed the storyline, flow, characters, and descriptions. **The book veers between exciting, sexy to spiritual. Loved it!**" Dr. Rajesh, Dental Surgeon, and Life Coach.

"Felt like reading more and more. There is **a lot of honesty,** and the **book was inspiring**. It was **Realistic with layers of depth. Thoroughly enjoyed reading** it. The **writing is pretty awesome, and the poems were a treat to read. Could relate to some of the stories in the book. The dialogues had truth to them!!** Keep it up, and I hope to read more books written by you!! Madhu, IT Professional.

"**Pearls of Wisdom.**' We expect a lot, a lot from ourselves, from our partners, from our children, from our colleagues, from our bosses, and who in the world could live up to our expectations when we ourselves were flawed? Surprisingly, we could easily see the flaws in others, but somehow, we were blinded to our own flaws.' You will find more of those pearls of wisdom. The book **portrays an honest journey into the inner secret cells of one's true self.** Asha - a doctor, a mother, a wife, a daughter, a **writer, a poet, a storyteller**, and most importantly, a woman - **unleashes some truths that may be difficult to swallow. But true life, as you already** know, is not like those flashy movies. Read this book without prejudice to find **yourself opening the doors to happiness and love. Don't be afraid to see some reflections!!!**" S.B, Cyber Security.

"**Very Well Written. I love how you say during your medical training, you dissected the human brain but didn't discuss how the mind works.** You mentioned that we are getting away from our core. I totally agree. That part about how such **high and false societal standards can make us "mere mortals" feel like derelicts...brilliant!** I totally agree we must redefine success from the big house/car material focus and include what makes us happy." Acupuncture Josh.

"**Unique**! Appreciate Dr. Menon's hard work and dedication to convey to readers about **the importance of peace of Mind in life** rather than the pressure to live the extraordinary life of glamour and wealth. **Dr. Menon's desire to help others by sharing her personal and professional experiences, to value life and relationships is well expressed in this book.** Few important points that help the readers to think intensely-- living with contentment, reap what you sow, the hope of eternity."Thank you, Dr. Menon Thomas Joseph, Nurse Practitioner.

"**Fascinating Journey of The Human Mind.** Hats off, Asha Menon. It was a pleasure reading your book. The book is **captivating.** The **language is lucid. You took the reader through the fascinating roller coaster journey of the human mind. Keep writing** and fascinating the reader with more perspectives and **insights into human life**: Ramdas P. Menon, Retired Banker.

"A physician by trade and a very creative soul. **I enjoyed it**, as she introduced us to **various characters and took us into their private lives!** Got to enjoy their travels **to places far away with descriptions that made me feel I was there myself!** Well Done, Dr. Menon!" Nilima, Life Coach.

"**Enjoyable storyline. Great work**, well written." Shantigram.

The author beautifully explains the importance of one's mind and thoughts through the characters' lives. **Highly recommend** this book." SA.

"**Great Book of Self-Discovery!** The **author is versatile in weaving one's journey from self-doubt, leading to confidence,** and learns to see the world from a spiritual point of view. **Well spun story** and characters are true to life." S L Narayana

Dedication

This Novel is dedicated to my parents. My father, fondly called K.Y, was a legend in his lifetime who instilled in me the love of literature. He introduced me to books in my childhood, bringing me the Enid Blyton series when he returned home after his tours and then helping me graduate to AJ Cronin, Somerset Maugham, and Boris Pasternak.

My mother, Ammu, a homemaker who prodded me to get a good education; for then, "I could be independent and not have to ask a man to buy me the things I wanted." She encouraged me to sing and write and surely is my greatest critic.

To my husband, who has held my hand through this journey.

To my friends Bushu and Meena, who read my manuscript and gave me the 'go-ahead' nod.

To my friends who have believed in my writing, my philosophy and requested me to write.

To all those writers before me who have inspired me.

"When I sit down to write a book, I don't say to myself; I'm going to produce a work of art. I write because there is some lie I want to expose, some fact to which I want to draw attention, and my initial concern is to get a hearing."
— George Orwell.

Table of Contents

Tame The Mind

Introduction

This book was conceived to give voice to the stress and sadness I saw all around me. Despite living in the United States of America, the wealthiest country in the world, I found a gnawing restlessness everywhere.

As a physician, people came to me for their physical illnesses. I do not know how and when it began, but over the years, I was counseling patients for their personal problems more than giving medications for their physical ailment. I was giving them insights into their issues and learning from them.

An undercurrent of stress consumed 80 percent of the people who walked through my doors. Marital problems, sexual problems, bad bosses, children feeling let down by their parents, parents feeling let down by their children— there was no dearth of reasons for all the frustration.

To me, as an outsider, some of them seemed to have everything going for them, yet they were unhappy. Even the wealthy were not immune to an undercurrent of dissatisfaction and mental anguish.

As an observer, listening to people, I felt most of the problems we faced were due to our thought process and how we perceived each other.

Most importantly, I found people lacked coping skills. No school taught this.

I had always been an avid reader and writer. As a thirteen-year-old, I had written a long letter to my uncle, who was the first person to tell me that I should become a writer.

Then life happened. I was a good student, and my father suggested that I apply to medical schools. I did just that and was admitted to a medical school at the age of 18.

Medicine engrossed me. I loved learning about the physiology of the human body and the intricate and meticulous functioning of every cell in the body. Each cell is a world of its own.

I must add; I was not too fond of anatomy; memorizing the names of the multitude of nerves and arteries as they coursed through our body was overwhelming.

In the anatomy class, where we dissected the brain and labeled every part of the brain, the mind, which was what guided us throughout our life, was not described.

This intangible thing called 'mind' was, in effect, non-existent in the anatomy class.

Through college and medical school, I would write poems, essays, stories, which my friends and family enjoyed; some of the materials were published in school and community magazines.

Last year, I was annoyed with myself for not having done anything with the stories I had written. One day, I spread all the manuscripts on my bed. As I looked at them, I felt these were human stories waiting to be told.

There were stories exploring love and sexuality. There were stories about the pitfalls of modern living. The pursuit of happiness as understood and pursued made people unhappy and not at peace with themselves. Within a week, I decided to publish them.

If the reader sees slices of life in the pages of this book, these are stories told to understand the fickleness of the human mind, why we behave in ways detrimental to our well-being. Stories related to lay bare some of the myths associated with love and sex.

Why the modern world, despite all its comforts and gadgets and being wealthier, than at any other time in history, stays stressed and unhappy across all strata of society?

This book is the culmination of that quest. It is written in the form of fiction, for in fiction, there is leeway to express oneself.

Every line in this book is written to convey something meaningful yet entertaining to the reader. It is a quick read. I deliberately made it so as this is the era of social media and distractions.

Every self-help book talked about success, but not many talked about the one thing that led to failure in life. If a person lacked this one thing, despite whatever money, fame, or glamor one had, real happiness would elude him or her.

Shattering the societal definition of success, changing the paradigm of success can help us be successful in the true sense and be genuinely at peace with ourselves. Worldly success does not always lead to fulfillment.

To understand the difference, please keep reading.

Prologue

Greed and Generosity will vie with each other.

Love and hate will lie beside each other.

Such is the human mind.

These are stories of human existence, stories of escape from the trappings of the human mind, from the tricks our mind plays with us.

We could imprison our minds with the shackles of our perceived inadequacy or liberate it from the chains holding us, from our diffidence, our fears, our insecurities—for the human mind can enchain the human psyche or emancipate it.

This book is about a woman's exploration of sexuality, relationships, and a quest to define happiness, what love means, what life means, and above all, what matters most.

Perhaps, not for the first time in a novel, the male protagonist and his dilemma as he cruises through life have been brought to light as 'men do not talk about their issues.'

The Rejected Husband

Neil entered his white picket fenced house; shoulders slumped on his tall, broad frame, briefcase in one hand, the evening shadow following him as he dragged his legs along the long-curved driveway. Fumbling for keys, he looked at his mansion with its three-car garage and immaculately manicured gardens located in the posh suburb of Warren, New Jersey. He felt no joy as he opened the front door and entered his home. Sonia, his wife, looked up, smiled at him, and went back to chatting with her friends on the phone.

"How was your day?" he asked her.

"It was all right," she answered absentmindedly.

Over the years, their conversations had plateaued. That night as most nights, they ate dinner in silence.

That night as most nights, he initiated the sex, fearing her moods, her rejection. Perhaps she was tired or had a confabulated headache. That night she acquiesced to his relief.

Sonia lay on her back, waiting for the sex to get over, her mind racing through the myriad chores she needed to get done the next morning. He knew as he had known through the ten years of their marriage that she was not present. He kissed her neck, her breasts, wanting some foreplay, all of which irked her.

"You looked ravishing in the green dress this morning," he said, hoping flattery and sweet talk would stimulate her.

She was pleased. "I am glad you find me pretty after ten years."

"Do you find me good-looking?" he enquired, needing some affirmations.

"I have never liked the thick lips and the paunch you have."

His libido began to ebb. "Is that why you don't like sex?" His voice quavered as he spoke.

She felt obliged to cajole the cry baby.

"Oh, come on." Placing her arms against his back, she cooed, "come inside me."

His erection had shriveled. He forced himself a few minutes later, thinking of a movie character he had found interesting—Mrs. Robinson.

He had to, to keep his sanity. His wife complied so as not to feel guilty. She did not want to deal with his sulks the next day.

The next morning the night was forgotten. As she brought him some tea, her sleep-drowned eyes enamored him. He loved her as he had when he had met her for the first time. He remembered the time when he had saved her from a few male friends who were determined to molest her. The damsel in distress and one of the prettiest girls in the university had fallen for this decent, will-be-there-for-her, caring, loving man who had rescued her from the wolves.

2

That night determined to rectify this flaw in their marriage, he blurted. "Shall we go for counseling?"

She was shocked. "For what?"

They had nice cars, a beautiful home, servants, and great careers. Above all, their friends envied them.

"Counseling to improve our sex lives," he muttered under his breath.

"I allow you anytime you want, don't I? My friend Sheela allows her husband to touch her just once a month."

"You don't seem interested anymore." He spoke softly, not wanting to seem accusatory.

"You get your orgasm. For me, sex doesn't matter much."

"I need you to respond, not just lie there." He did accuse, trembling.

"After ten years, kids, responsibilities, sex is not the most important thing on my mind."

Neil kept quiet. He hated for the war of words to escalate. They turned their backs to each other. He tossed and turned, covering his ears as he heard her sleep-ridden rhythmic breathing.

The creaking of the bed woke her up. He was jerking himself off with a seminude photo of a woman on his cell phone.

She was disgusted. Huffing and puffing, she took her pillows and scooted to an empty bedroom.

"Pervert," she mumbled.

He heard her. "It is better than having sex with you," he screamed.

They did not talk to each other for days, and needless to say, they did not have sex either. A few nights later, Sonia felt the need to break the ice, which was getting thick. She wanted to keep the marriage intact. She cared for him. She wanted to preserve the facade of a happy marriage. More importantly, she did not want her friends judging her, whispering to each other, 'All that glitters is not gold.' No, she could not bear that. She would keep the marriage intact, she thought, but at her terms.

"Come on, Neil, let's have sex today." He welcomed the attempt. The house was beginning to seem dead and cold. They made their way to the bedroom. Sonia hugged him. "Come on, baby," she said. He started kissing her lips. She tolerated. When he went down on her, in an attempt to pleasure her, he asked, "Do you like it?"

"Come inside," came the curt reply.

He came inside her, spent.

She was glad the ice had melted, and all would be the same again.

The Wedding Anniversary

The car came to a dead end. Neil looked around angrily and honked at the indifferent kids playing on the street.

His head seemed to be exploding, dreading the nights. It all seemed unfair when Sonia seemed so content.

Sonia was a dutiful wife. The auburn hair—silhouetting her smooth, pale face, curled onto the shoulders of her tall, petite figure. She had small, slightly slanted eyes. Her best feature was the perfectly straight nose, which made her strikingly photogenic. She usually posed for photographs with her head slightly turned to a side, her chin somewhat raised, to accentuate her straight nose. When they walked hand in hand, heads turned.

"Smile," she told Neil as they entered the banquet hall.

It was their friend's first wedding anniversary. Lights glittered all around. The dais was decorated with real flowers, and the air felt fresh as the sweet scent of jasmine whiffed through the house.

Sonia took a deep breath, taking in the fragrance, the changing colorful strobe lights, the balloons floating in the air, the chandeliers, and the pink and white flowers on the table. Above all, she was happy that she and Neil were walking hand in hand, and the world would continue to think that they were a happy couple.

Sammy, her friend, approached them. "I saw your vacation pictures on Facebook. You guys look so happy together." Looking at Neil, she added, "I envy her. You take her everywhere."

Neil smiled uncomfortably.

When one is at a loss for words, a smile is perhaps an apt reply.

"Oh, come, I have to show you something." Sammy took Sonia's hand and wheeled her away to show off the expensive jewelry she had bought that month.

Neil, not having anything better to do, headed for the appetizers, checking the platter of food, decided to go for the baked chicken puffs. He was relishing the warm crunchiness when he heard a voice behind him.

"A bit lost, aren't you," he heard a somewhat familiar female voice. He turned around to find himself looking at a long-lost schoolmate of his.

"Sylvia!" he exclaimed.

The sudden revival of old friendships always brings a lot of cheer in one's heart.

The moroseness Neil was feeling diminished. He hugged Sylvia. "God, how many years has it been, and look at you," he was wondering whether to articulate the truth.

She helped him. "Stop. I have aged, and I have let go of myself. But you look young and handsome as ever."

He hid any surprise he felt at those remarks. "Really?" he questioned, checking his reflection in the brass cabinet.

"You surely have stood the test of time," she laughed.

His wife's comments about his lips and paunch resonated against Sylvia's remarks. He was eager to know more about Sylvia's opinion of him and fervently wanted to continue talking to her.

They spent the next fifteen minutes learning about what each was doing.

She was an assistant professor on the tenure track. Hesitantly, she added, "I have a career, but my personal life is in shambles." I divorced my husband recently," she remarked.

Neil waited for the 'why.' His eyebrows raised into an implicit question mark.

"He was cheating on me."

"Oh!" Came Neil's empathetic exclamation.

'Oh' at times is a befitting reply when one wants to avoid a factual one.

"What have you been up to?" Sylvia asked.

As he was formulating a reply, Sonia butted in, dragging Neil away.

"I want you to meet some VIPs."

"Sonia, this is..."

Later, they are leaving. They are influential people, and I want you to meet them." He was pulled away. Somehow 'influential people' had not meant much to him. Feigning interest, he patiently made small talk while getting restless to return to authenticity.

Sonia was exuberant. Words of flattery found their way out of her mouth. 'This was the moment she would use all her charms to help Neil climb the ladder.' She shrugged away the uneasy thought that Neil was not an ambitious corporate climber. She bit her tongue, annoyed at him. He tried his best not to display irritation.

That night he told her he was tired and went to bed.

The Long Night

The night seemed long. The initial heady days of romance had not prepared Neil for the domestication of his romantic dreams, these unromantic nights. 'Did most women not prioritize sex? Were they frigid, asexual?' The movies never indicated that. Most books written, most films made had a man and a woman falling in love and living happily ever after. Sex was depicted as an out-of-this-world experience if the movies and books were to be believed. He was eager for answers. He did not have any female friends. He thought of Sylvia, whom he had abandoned unceremoniously at the party. 'Wonder if she cares about sex?' he thought.

Sylvia was some years his junior at school. He had noticed some gray strands in her chestnut brown hair. There were a few crows' feet at the corners of her eyes when she smiled. He wondered why they were called crow's-feet. Sylvia was slender with a sculpturesque figure and shapely legs. Her large, dewy eyes, which exuded a certain calmness, reminded him of a tranquil lake—her lips reminded him of soft flower petals. She was not a beauty but not unattractive either.

Neil found his musings entertaining him. He would call her tomorrow. That was the first thought that gave him solace that night.

He got up, a bit groggy after an almost sleepless night, wishing he had had sex with his wife and slept off the night. Maybe he was expecting too much from life, from his wife.

He had missed the alarm. As he rushed to get ready for work, he saw breakfast laid out on the table with a note. 'Enjoy the toast and marmalade. The orange juice is in the fridge—hot tea in the flask. I have an early breakfast meeting with the team today. Didn't want to wake you. Bye.' Love Sonia.

The Crush

Neil grabbed the toast, got into his car. 'The traffic in the city was getting bad to worse. Why was it so slow?' he cursed.

The theory of relativity must be acknowledged here. It always took him forty minutes to reach the workplace. Today the forty minutes did not seem to arrive soon enough.

Julia, his twenty-two-year-old secretary, smiled at him as he barged through the double doors. "You are late for the meeting."

"Tell me something I don't already know," he barked.

"Sorry, sir, but the VP has closed all access to the meeting," she was apologetic.

He grunted at her and walked to his office.

"Shall I get you some coffee?" he heard her say. She was trying to make amends.

"It is not your fault." He emphasized on the word fault. "But, the coffee would be good."

She knew he liked it light with two creamers and half a teaspoon of sugar. He took a sip savoring it. She waited to find out if he liked it.

"Good."

She was pleased. Now she could get on with her work.

"Do you have a boyfriend?"

"Yes," she replied, wondering why he had asked that. He had never really cared about her personal life.

"How is he?" That was too general a question. "Do you love him?"

"I suppose so."

He looked at her quizzically, raising his eyebrows. "Are you planning to get married?"

"We have been living together for the past two years, and we are planning marriage by the end of next year."

"Are you sure?"

Now it was Julia's turn to look quizzically and raise her eyebrows.

"You just said you are not sure if you love him." He felt the need to defend himself and refrained from asking the one question that was on his mind. 'How is the sex?' Luckily, another way of asking the same question hit him like a bolt. "Are you two compatible... I mean in bed?"

It was the time of the #Me Too movement, and as Neil uttered these questions, he regretted them. He was not sure how these words would be construed. 'Invading my privacy, asking intimate questions, asking unwarranted questions, making me uncomfortable, asking questions unrelated to work or plain sexual harassment.'

"I am sorry. I didn't mean to ask you that. My friend's son is researching female sexuality, and we were discussing this last night, and I blurted a question from his questionnaire. I hope you understand." And as if the concocted on the spur explanation was not enough, he added timidly, "I hope I have not offended you in any way."

"You have not, sir. I have known you for the last three years. You have been a great mentor and very kind to me, sir."

As he heaved a sigh of relief, she went on, "How is your sex life? Is it fulfilling?"

He stared at her. He wanted to say, 'I am your boss, and you have no right to ask me such things.' He had needed to vent his bottled frustrations. He had not been able to divulge this raw area, which perturbed him, to his male friends.

Men only talked about their conquests. He would appear too much of a failure. He could hear their laughter deafening him.

A shrink might give him medications for the depression, which was beginning to engulf him. He knew the exact cause of his misery, and he knew the cure. The cure he despaired of attaining because even though all the self-help books mentioned that we had the power to change our lives, his antidote depended on another, the woman he had taken as his wife.

"It is horrible." Stooping onto the table, he covered his face with his palms. 'There it was. Now she would tell the whole office, and he would be the laughingstock—this man who had seemed to have everything squared.'

He felt a hand on his shoulder. He looked up to find Julia standing very close to him, patting him gently. Her breasts would touch his face if he looked up anymore. He dared not, hoping she would go away and wishing she would not. For the first time, he became aware of her sexuality. She had always been this mechanically servile lady who brought him coffee, informed him about the day's appointments, canceling them, and rescheduling them at his beck and call. Here she was, pacifying him.

He had bared his vulnerabilities to this young woman whose skin was smooth, whose face was covered with a thick layer of foundation—the well fitted artificial eyelashes enhanced her green eyes, which revealed no crows' feet. Her thin lips shone with lip gloss. Youth had made her flaws inconsequential, and she had the body of a woman whose contours were not lost to pregnancy.

His hands trembled; his lips quivered at the thought of having her. She was aware of the want in his eyes. He was the epitome of all that she admired. He had a master's degree, was a tall, dark, charming man with high cheekbones, a chiseled jawline which enhanced his straight nose, whose steel-gray eyes focused on getting work done. A quiet yet approachable man, he was gentle yet demanding of his subordinates. She had never seen him raise his voice.

People respected him.

She respected him.

Neil had seemed to have it all. How misled most of us could be. Here he was, disclosing his innermost secret to his

14

secretary. She was secretly elated to be the chosen one. Somehow vulnerability and grief when shared, created, or exalted friendships.

That night when Julia's boyfriend made love, she imagined her boss on top of her kissing her gently with his luscious lips, his seemingly taut belly, thrusting his virility into her. And she came like never before.

The next morning for the first time, she looked forward to going to work. She frantically rummaged through her closet, deciding what to wear. A tight blouse with a slightly low cut? She did not want to appear too obvious or trashy. She chose a rose-tinted top. It reflected well on the pallid skin of her youthful face. She glowed with love, love for this wiser, older man.

She waited for him to enter through the double doors, nervous, holding her belly in an attempt to calm and be free of the fluttering butterflies churning at the thought of seeing him. Finally, her knight in shining armor arrived, and time stood still. She smiled, coyly acknowledging their shared secret. The secret of his asexual marriage and her love for him. She would give him her body and soul, make him happy, wipe his tears away.

"Shall I bring you some coffee?" She asked, getting close to him, waiting to see his lips quiver, his hands tremble with want for her.

"I am fine. I don't want coffee. It is time for the board room meeting with the vice president." He said in a business-like tone.

Her mouth went dry. Her throat made some noise as she swallowed her spit, rudely awakened from her reverie.

She went on with her mundane work expecting to hear Neil's voice with every phone call. He did not call, and her heart sank into a bottomless abyss, the wait unbearable.

As Julia was leaving after a long day had gone wrong, Neil came up to her workstation. Her heart stopped. The world stopped. He would say, 'I love you' and take her. She would love him back ardently, and all would be well. This day with all the upheavals, the wait, the emotional roller-coaster would be erased forever. He would be hers, and she his.

"Maria has been appointed as my new secretary. She has been working at the company for over thirty years and was my secretary before you joined. If you wish to continue working for the company, then Rusty will be more than happy to have you work as his secretary."

She was silent, disappointment cloaked in a steel veil over her unfazed face.

As she drove home that evening, tears fell off her face. She blinked to clear her eyes of the blurriness.

As she entered her one-bedroom apartment, she saw her boyfriend lounging on the sofa, bottles of whiskey and pizza on the table. He had gotten the pizza from the pizzeria where he worked as a cashier. "Been waiting for you, munchkin. It is hot," he pointed towards his genitals. He was sweaty, red, and drunk. She suppressed an urge to vomit.

Love or Respect

After a week of their meeting, Neil found the courage to call Sylvia. He had been debating the opening line. 'Called you just to say hi, called you to apologize for leaving you stranded at the party as my wife dragged me away to meet with the VIPs.' He was inclined towards the latter. The phone rang, putting a hold on his thoughts. It was Sylvia. He was relieved about not having to find an excuse to call her.

"You deserted me and took off with your wife." Sylvia's voice was exuberant. For a moment, Neil was puzzled. She was referring to 'that' uncomfortable moment last week.

"So sorry about last week. I meant to call you and apologize."

"Really," came the retort. Next time you want to apologize or intend to call me, just do so. You are safe." 'Safe,' he was not sure what she meant. Maybe this was some kind of reassurance during the '#Me Too' movement.

He felt glad to have found a safe friend, especially a safe female friend, during these times. He now felt so secure that he asked her out without thinking, without blinking. "Would you like to have some coffee after work? I can pick you up." He was confident she wouldn't misconstrue the pickup phrase nor his intentions. He wanted to uncover myths about female sexuality, and in the process, perhaps salvage his own. He was nervous and excited at the same time. A voice in his head cautioned him, 'I should pop this question, not at first but the next rendezvous. He didn't want to scandalize her.'

Neil felt anxious as he carefully chose a cozy restaurant far away from his home and work. Sylvia greeted him with a smile as she got into his car. He wished she were more attractive, maybe colored her hair with those fashionable highlights, and didn't wear the baggy clothes, which seemed to be a norm with her. "We can go to the Trilleca," trying to impress her with an expensive high-end restaurant in New York City. Most women would have summed him up as a well-to-do, suave man who enjoyed elegance and was generous enough to treat others to it. He had not cared, but the women he knew did. He was not sure why he felt the need to impress her. He was roused from his preoccupation.

"Never heard of the Trilleca," she said.

He suppressed an urge to raise his eyebrows.

"Are you in the mood for some Thai, Chinese, Indian, Mexican, or Italian?"

Cuisines of the hundred and ninety-five countries of the world could be grouped into five or six main courses.

"All I want is to go home, put my feet up, eat some home-cooked baked fish with piping hot lentil soup."

He wondered what would impress her. 'Surely restaurants were not her thing; clothes and hair dyes were not either. Had her husband left her because of this?'

"Would you rather go home?" Neil asked as politely as he could muster.

"Sounds great. Why don't we go over to my place?"

He blinked, 'wondering if this was an invitation.' Surely, she didn't make it seem like that. It was just one safe woman inviting one safe man into her bachelor pad to share their common childhood nightmares. He agreed, pleased that it would save him a long drive through the city traffic.

New York

New York was a maze of roads. Once an exit was missed, it took that much longer to get to the destination. The peak hour with impatient drivers added to the commotion. Drivers seemed to be in a hurry, speeding only to be slowed down by accidents caused by life's need to rush. Also, the Trilleca was way too expensive, even by New York standards. That was money saved. A restaurant surrounded by strangers hardly seemed a place to probe into female sexuality.

"Turn right, turn right," she shrieked, not wanting him to lose his way.

Twenty minutes later, they were at her apartment complex. She swiped open the lobby door, pressed the elevator button. He followed her into the elevator, which stopped on the fifteenth floor. As he stepped out, the view of New York with its well-lit skyscrapers kissing the clouds exhilarated him. The skyline was studded with beautiful buildings, some boastful of architectural splendor—others were regular box-shaped buildings where aesthetics had not only been compromised by economics but also by sheer indifference.

Neil was relieved not to be driving in circles trying to locate a parking spot in downtown New York City. Above all, he was happy that the prying eyes of strangers would not be on him as he sought answers to his dilemma.

As she unlocked her apartment door, he mentally convinced himself. 'They were both safe, and he was merely rekindling an old friendship. Thank God she was not his type. His very next thought was, 'who was his type? His wife, who dressed impeccably, wore the 'Sakki' designer, burnt credit cards. Thank God it was her credit card.' He had decided not to indulge her early on in their marriage. She loved to show off her bags, one for every attire with shoes in tow. Once at a fundraiser for orphans, she was seated next to the philanthropic wife of a millionaire, and he had heard her say, "this dress cost me three thousand dollars." He had rolled his eyes and left her with the philanthropic wife of the millionaire as the philanthropic wife of the millionaire refilled her glass of wine twice, appalled. Again, he reminded himself, Sonia loved to cook, made him tasty delicacies, kept the house tidy all this while working at a corporate job she hated. Well, she had the right to indulge in designers and brands. If only she loved him the way he desired her, it would be perfect, and the vagaries could be forgiven.

Does God always keep something away from us so that we reach out to him all the time?

Sylvia came out of the shower, her hair tied in a ponytail, wearing a tank top and a flowy ankle-length skirt. There was a hint of maroon lipstick on her face, which he had not noticed earlier.

She sat on the sofa facing him. "Tea or wine?"

He was not sure. It seemed a bit too early for wine. He opted for tea.

"So, tell me, how is life?"

'Was she just as interested in probing into his psyche as he was?' "It has been alright."

"You have a good job, money, a beautiful home, and a pretty wife. You must be pleased as punch?" Well, she had numerically rattled out why a man having all of the above ingredients should be buoyant with happiness.

He was not interested in talking about himself, and it would be too early to disillusion her. "How has your life been?"

She laughed, her perfectly well-aligned pearly white teeth sparkling at him. "You are a parrot. You just parroted my words."

"Go on, why did you divorce your husband," he jumped to the question impatiently.

"He fell out of love with me and went for a much younger woman but uglier." She was not sure why she felt compelled to add the word uglier.

"Beauty is skin deep, but ugliness can be bone-deep," he quipped jovially. "How was the sex?" He had not meant to pop the question so soon, but there it was. He twiddled his thumb while waiting and wondering how she would react?

21

"Sex was good. Our needs matched in the initial days of courtship and marriage. Now that I am single, I cover myself in rags and bags to avoid male attention. No unwanted men," she reiterated.

'Was that a warning to him,' he wondered. "I thought sex was the most important reason people divorced over."

"Sex and money," she replied. "The two nouns that can drag a relationship down into a chasm and, of course, chronic abuse of any kind." There she had summed up the three reasons for divorce.

"What about falling out of love," he was curious.

"Love is overrated. If you respect each other, love should resurface even if it has ebbed. The keyword is respect."

"And love?" he queried.

"You are a romantic," she laughed. Neil could see her cleavage and desperately tried to look away. She noticed him looking away and was pleased. With a smile on her lips, she dished out some fish, salads, and some lentil soup to go with it, inviting him to the dining table.

"Oh, I don't want to impose on you."

"Nonsense, help yourself. I am not a great cook, but I can fend for myself, and, as you can see, I can toss a meal together," she smirked. "So, tell me about yourself. How is your marriage?"

"It's ok, I suppose."

"Do you love her?"

"Yes, I suppose."

"Are you never sure of yourself?" She asked peevishly, clearly agitated with his not sure lines.

We hardly sleep together," he blurted.

Erectile Dysfunction

Sylvia stared through the window, not knowing how to react. Neil was looking for answers, and she was a bit embarrassed to pursue the conversation. "Why?" She finally managed to break the silence.

"I think my wife is frigid. Do you find me attractive?"

"Of course, you are," she replied as she took in his thick mop of hair carefully brushed in place, his broad frame, and if he had a paunch, it was well hidden under the loose shirt. It was his turn to be pleased.

"Sylvia, my self-confidence is low and has been ebbing. Of late, I have been suffering from erectile dysfunction. My head and body feel like they want to explode."

"I believe you have been personalizing your wife's lack of interest as a sign of your inadequacy."

"You talk like a therapist."

She smiled, trying to ease the air. She had not parroted every word of his. 'My head and body feel like they want to explode. I haven't made love in two years. No man has touched me in two years, and I am scared of being hurt.'

She remained quiet.

"It is getting late. Go home before your wife reports you missing."

Sylvia went to bed happy that night. She had found a friend, that too, a male friend who had revealed his innermost debacle to her.

That night she wrote in her diary:

Men rarely shared their emotions with others. They discussed their conquests but not their failure. They discussed sports and politics but not what bothered them. They did not discuss their wives but tooted their girlfriends, even so, more about the quantity than quality. They were different.

Don't Feel Like Going Home

A few weeks went by, and Neil was getting restless. He had not heard from Sylvia. He enjoyed her company. She was cerebral, or so he thought. She did not seem interested in shoes or bags like most of the women he knew. He decided he would call her today, just to talk.

She answered on the first ring. "Why haven't you called me?" she demanded.

He was slightly taken aback but pleased all the same. He was glad that Sylvia's eagerness to connect with him mirrored his own.

"I am coming over," he said.

'Waiting," came her reply. She hurriedly tidied her apartment, lighted the scented candles, dimmed the incandescent lights, threw her baggy work clothes in the washer—rummaging through the wardrobe, she could not find anything to wear. She wanted to dress for him. She wanted to feel desired by him. As she desperately searched for the appropriate attire, she found the blue shirt and the dark blue skirt she had worn a few days into her marriage. The blue had enhanced her smooth olive skin. She had glanced at the mirror and smiled at her reflection. The blouse draped her firm and full breasts—the skirt fit her well, enhancing her tiny waist, uncovering her long shapely legs.

As she had headed out to work, her husband had grabbed her slender body, kissed her while pouring words of love: "You are every man's dream. I cannot take my eyes off your face; how can I look anywhere else?" That day, before leaving for work, they had made love desperate and hungry.

Absentmindedly she wore the blue shirt and the dark blue knee-length skirt, wondering why things had gone so wrong. Sitting on the bed, she was not sure if she missed John, her ex-husband, or missed being married. She brushed off a tear as she heard the doorbell.

"Come in," she said, opening the door for Neil. There was no welcoming smile on her face.

Neil walked in, momentarily stunned at her transformation. Her colored hair was wavy, contouring her oval face and neck. The large sensitive eyes placed symmetrically on her face reminded him of a dove—her long and curved eyelashes needed no mascara.

"You look pretty," he remarked.

There was still no smile. "I have some tea ready for you." She poured him and herself some tea and sat facing him, he on the bigger couch and she on a single sofa.

"You seem upset. What's up, something bothering you?"

She was glad that he had, at the least, guessed. John would never have surmised or cared if she were upset. "I was thinking about my marriage, rather the deterioration of my marriage."

His ears perked up. This is what he had wanted to hear. Conversing with Sylvia was so easy.

"I think I was always trying to change him. He would never clean up after he shaved or ate. He was messy, and I kept nagging him."

"Surely, that couldn't have been a reason for annulment?"

She continued, ignoring Neil's interruption. "If he were late, it would upset me, and I reacted by throwing tantrums. It was my way of letting him know that I missed him like a child cries when needing attention, but I never told him that I missed him. I didn't want him to feel powerful in the marriage."

"Marriages can be a power struggle," he consoled, thinking of his own need to make sure he was the man of the house—he wanted everybody to adhere to his will. His mother had been docile and had obeyed his father. That is what he had seen and learned to expect. "For Sonia, it is her way or the highway."

It was the first time in the few weeks since their meeting; he had mentioned his wife by name. The mention of his wife jolted Sylvia. He had a life other than hers, and she must stay away from him; she made a mental note.

"Did you seek counseling?"

"We did." The psychiatrist labeled him with a diagnosis, which John did not believe to be accurate, and the psychologist had some bookish knowledge but no worldly wisdom. We quit counseling. John refused to continue the medication. It was turning him into a zombie."

"Did you talk to friends or family?"

"Neil, there are very few people you can talk to about your intimate torments."

"You can talk to me," he encouraged.

27

"For the first time that day, she touched his hand, tenderly, and smiled. Her pearly white teeth captured his attention again. "Thank you, Neil."

"No, no. Thank you, Sylvia."

"Shall I get you some fish and salad?"

'Did she eat the same thing every day?' He wondered. Well, it was tasty, and for him, it was a change from the spaghetti and meatballs he ate.

"I have some sautéed mixed vegetables stewed in coconut curry," she added.

"Can't wait," came the prompt reply.

They made small talk as they ate. Neil did not feel like going home that night.

He called his wife, "I will be extremely late tonight. There is a deadline. Must submit the report. I may stay at a hotel."

Sonia, his wife, knew all about corporate deadlines. She herself had stayed many a time, at her desk working, into the wee hours of the morning—the next day directing all her pent-up frustrations with her job towards Neil, finding fault with every action of his. He had many a time stayed back at work too.

"Ok, see you. I will be home in two days. Going to Connecticut tomorrow," she replied.

He was pleased. "See you when you are back."

Sylvia, cutting some fruits for dessert, was quiet.

"Sorry, have I taken too much liberty? I didn't even ask you if I could stay back here tonight."

"You don't feel like going home," she quizzed.

"I don't feel like," Neil admitted sheepishly. The flames from the candle were flickering. "Give me your hand," he said, sitting across the table. She extended her palm with the knife in it.

"Oh, no. Keep the knife away." He went and sat on the floor of the living room. She joined him on the floor. "Give me your hand." This time she put her empty hand in his. He dragged her closer to him. She felt giddy.

The Love Affair

Neil kissed her, and Sylvia was aroused like never before. She kissed him back, passionately. He had forgotten the feeling of being kissed—the fervent kisses stimulated every inch of his body. Her lips knew no limits, and her teeth bit his skin, flaming him. He was hard, rock hard, to his surprise. She rode him, and as he hit her insides, she screamed and fell on his chest, spent.

Suddenly, what the movies had shown and the books had written about love and lovemaking seemed somewhat real.

She had validated the invalid in him through her need for him, to touch him and be touched by him.

An affair had begun. Neil felt alive. A song on his lips, he went about his work, accompanied his wife to the parties she had arranged, bought his wife clothes, jewelry, and whatever she asked of him. Once or twice a month, he would sleep with his wife. He had no expectations, and hence, he was hardly ever disappointed. Slowly and gradually, he stopped these encounters with his wife, and she never questioned him. She was glad he was getting old just as she was.

One day a year later, when autumn was starting to glide in, and the green leaves were turning into a myriad of colors—the colors of heaven seemed to descend on earth, Sylvia and Neil were lying on her bed watching the full moon starting to peek from behind the clouds. The city lights blazed from the windows in a frenzy as dusk fell.

He had come a bit early during their lovemaking. Sylvia was not perturbed. Many a time, he came prematurely; spent and tired, he had dozed off immediately. As he slept, she looked at him tenderly and wrote:

An orgasm was a man's privilege. For the woman, it could be hit or miss, and sometimes it did not seem to matter as long as there was love, and she yearned for his touch.

There were some days when they lay next to each other, her arm on his chest and her leg folded on his thigh. On those days, orgasm was a faraway thought—they just enjoyed each other, conversed with each other, content in their love for each other.

"Neil, I was walking in the park earlier today watching the birds, and the bees, the colors of the trees, were mirthfully reflected in the pond on one end of the expansive park. I felt I was the luckiest person in the world. I think I had a Tryst with God. Read this." She handed him the essay she had written about her experience that autumn day.

Tryst With God

My Tryst with God.

Yes, it was a day to reckon with.

I was eager to soak in the sun, take a walk in the park.

The boyfriend was busy meeting deadlines; the family was away taking care of their lives.

My ever-dependable girlfriends had missed my endearing phone calls.

So hesitantly, I ventured out alone. I took a deep intoxicating breath. I could not but smile.

I had ventured out alone, something I had always dreaded and hardly ever done before.

The ducks were floating in the lake, creating calm ripples.
The geese were flying in hordes above the water, babbling, territorial, and aggressive. A few birds with a silvery sheen against the bright blue sky were diving into the water, splashing and rippling the calm lake.

I continued my journey.

On my left was a young mother wheeling her child. The child squealed as I smiled at her. She was curious, secure in her mother's presence, welcoming, pure, and joyous, untainted by the complexities of adults.

I continued sprinting.

On my right was a middle-aged lady wheeling her invalid, old mother. The mother smiled at me through her weary eyes. I smiled back.

I had just witnessed the circle of life.

The sun was soaking me in its warmth, the wind playing with my hair, the light breeze caressing my face gently, reassuring me.

As I gazed at the hill, I realized 'I was alone but not lonely.'

I looked up at the deep blue sky. There were no dark clouds on the horizon.

The trees seemed to be waving at me. The golden yellow scorched autumn leaves, the mild mauve ones, the lustrous pink ones, the red-hot blazing leaves were mesmerizing me, beckoning.

Yes, Nature, God, Universe, whatever name I chose was in front of me, glorious in its abundance. I was in communion with The Lord.

'I walked alone but was not lonely.'

I must do this more often. Walk alone, together, hand in hand with God.

This was my 'Tryst with God.' And I knew I would never be lonely.

Cellulite And Men

"You are a fine writer. You should keep writing," Neil encouraged Sylvia.

"Thank you. When you say such things, I love you even more. Will you marry me?" she murmured, kissing his cheek.

He was not expecting this question. He fumbled, racking his brain for a politically correct answer. He had a wife who made him a lovely home and a lover who was ardent, intelligent, and attractive. Her cellulite and stretch marks had not bothered him. Her mind and body intrigued him.

Sylvia had once asked him, "Does my cellulite bother you?"

He must have overlooked them. He had not noticed them until she brought it to his attention. "Men usually don't care about cellulite or stretch marks even as women fret over it. Women are vain," he had laughed. He had grabbed her and uttered the words, "I love you the way you are."

"These words are an aphrodisiac for a woman," she had said, winking at him. She remembered how her ex-husband, John, had rolled his eyes at every opinion of hers.

A Broken Marriage

John, Sylvia's ex-husband, was short and stout. He had inherited the blue eyes from his German mother and dark hair from his Spanish father. John and Sylvia had dated for over two years before getting married. She had noticed him getting angry at the waiter in the restaurant and at strangers. He had remained attentive to her, and she had neglected his misgivings. He was a trader on Wall Street. She knew his work to be stressful and had felt the need to accommodate his every need and frenzy. There were nights he would keep awake with aggression and angst, and she would too, soothing him.

Six months into their marriage, he was on prescription stimulants.

Six months into their marriage, he found fault with everything she did.

Six months into their marriage, she was no longer turned on by him.

"You are not good toward me during the day. You get annoyed all the time. How do you expect me to switch on and be ready for you at night?" Sylvia told him one day when he made advances toward her.

"Just as I am ready for you at night?" John replied.

"John, I am a woman. It is not just about the act for me. It is a package. It comes with respect, love, kindness, and caring. You seem to have lost all that."

"Well, you must have made me lose all that. Sometimes you can take the blame too."

"Do you love me?" Sylvia questioned.

"I bring in so much money so we can live well."

"Money is not everything, John."

"Then what is?"

"Kind words."

"Do something I like so that I can be kind to you."

He retorted, not spelling out exactly what he wanted.

She could not read his mind. She did not understand where she was going wrong, and he was unable to clarify.

Sex became impossible between them. He drifted towards prostitutes. They were easier, prettier, well-endowed, and eager to please him. He had the money, and he secretly enjoyed hurting his wife.

Seven years into their marriage, he was elated to find his new, beautiful, and young intern lavishing attention on him.

His bruised ego needed repair.

She stroked it even more.

She wanted a rich man.

He wanted a trophy wife.

It was settled. Sylvia would be given enough money to live by. He would marry this young girl.

Sylvia did not object. She was happy to be rid of him. She did not contest in the courts. She just did not want him in her life anymore.

Adultery, A Two-Way Track

Sylvia had not mourned the deterioration of her marriage or John's infidelities. She was attracted to other men, and her husband had been too busy to notice. There had been discreet affairs.

One was with a man a few years younger than her. Through him, she had learned about her sexuality, that she was a woman with malice towards none, that she was sweet and gentle and generous. She had given him $10,000 to buy a home. A few months later, he had asked her for some more money, and this time she made some excuse. She decided not to be sponged by this young man; the risk, of course, would be losing him. He had continued to make love to her zealously, never tiring of telling her how beautiful she was. He was enthralled by her beauty and had rapturously kissed every part of her face enthusing between kisses that she mesmerized him. She basked in his enthrallment. He had made her fall in love with herself.

It was the first time she had come to know and see herself as attractive, an attribute she had never attributed to herself. She looked at herself in the mirror, and through him, found herself beautiful inside and out.

He even liked her nose, which was strange to her. Till his evaluation, she had always felt her nose to be stubby.

Sometimes we realize our worth through someone else. Sometimes we lose our self-worth through others as well.

His exuberance, his sexuality enamored her. His eyes lit up when he saw her. He had not been able to conceal the smile, the joy, the pride he had felt when they were having their first lunch together.

She had been amused to see the joy on his face as he looked at her. There was a childlike apparentness about him. Nothing hidden, nothing subdued, nothing suppressed, and there was no agenda. He had courted her; he had not manipulated or seduced her.

It had taken a few more meetings; the admiration in his eyes for her was unmistaken when the amusement she had felt gave way to intoxication. He talked nineteen to the dozen, had strong opinions, and enjoyed taking her everywhere. The motorbike ride was one of the most exhilarating rides of her life. Her hair, flying in the wind, she leaned her head on his shoulders as he drove her around the exciting new towns. He made her feel spectacular.

Their sexual escapades were filled to the brim with desire for each other. Their eyes were joyous at the sight of the other in a crowd. She hated the times he slept while she was awake, needing the constant interaction, his eagerness for her reflected in his eyes. The fervor and passion, the need to be touched by him, surpassed any other feeling.

She wrote in her diary:

Such is the deep feeling of love when combined with passion and fervor. The pull, the yearning, the smiling eyes locked together, the caressing in unforbidden public places somehow added to the thrill.

Through him, she knew her beauty, and through the coming years, her effect on men.

When he left to get married, her heart ached. He kept coming to her every so often, telling her only she could fulfill him.

One day he got a job in San Francisco. She accepted her fate.

He called her many a time. "I am just not able to love my wife the way I love you."

She wanted him to be happy. She stopped accepting his calls. She was over him.

The Bipolar Manic-Depressive

Sylvia's second lover was manic-depressive. She did not know it then, but many years later was able to connect the traits.

One day out of the blue, he had shouted at her as she was getting into her car at the shopping mall while people stared at them. "You rich professional women are so self-centered." She was confused. She had not the slightest idea as to what had triggered his wrath. She went home, flustered and miserable. Something was not fitting into her notion of normalcy.

A few weeks later, when he tried to make love to her, he told her, "You are this bombshell of a woman, and I feel terrible because I suffer from erectile dysfunction, and I've known that since my teens when I had slept with a willing maidservant at our home."

She had not cared. The orgasm had not mattered. The foreplay was what mattered. His eagerness for her was what mattered. His cooing kind, flattering but heartfelt words about his need for her, about her beauty, was what mattered. His desire for her was what mattered.

For a man, orgasm is the ultimate affirmation, erectile dysfunction being the worst curse.

He was acutely depressed at his inability to perform and had been chronically depressed since his teens.

A few weeks later, he invited himself to her house. She prepared an elaborate dinner, the aroma of spices blended with flowery fragrance. Sylvia wore a flattering-floral frock. Someone had told her that the dress made her look younger, almost like a college freshman.

Somehow the clothes we wear have a way of reflecting our moods.

She swirled around, holding the edges of her frock on either side, enjoying her appearance in the mirror. The thought of him kissing her brought a song to her lips. She waited for him. It was 6 pm, an hour went by, and then two hours, her desperation scorched the fire in her. She ached for him. Every minute seemed like an eternity. Her desire for him increased exponentially with the wait; her mind was exponentially agitated. He had not called her. It was 11 pm, and she felt deep despair. Every sound made her imagine this tall man with broad shoulders and impeccable features set on his square face pervade the house with his boyish charm, walking stealthily towards her holding her with passion as he had done a few nights ago. She wanted to be loved by him more than anything else that evening. He never came. As the orange twilight turned mauve and the colors fleeted through the trees welcoming the dusk, her heart sank into a pit, less at her loss but more at his loss, regretting the lost moment. He had not seen her in all her glory and will never know the overwhelming desire she had felt for him. The pangs subsided; she called his sister. "Oh, he's here at our place," she answered Sylvia's query. "Do you want to talk to him?"

"No," Sylvia said as she kept the phone down. It was his loss. It was her loss too. The moment of desire squished, quelled, and trampled upon. She removed her dress and the light makeup, changed into her pajamas, feeling numb. She went to the washroom, slowly washing away the lightly dusted powder from her face, removing the lipstick which she had applied so artistically to bring out the contours of her lips, remembering his remark, 'your lips remind me of the cupid's bow.' As tears fell, the mascara she had so painstakingly but unwillingly applied formed a thick layer of soot on her face. She scrubbed her face, removing every stain as if trying to erase him and the humiliation with this maneuver. She was scraping off the endearing, sweet nothings he had whispered in her ears.

He had stood her up, and she did not even want to know why.

A few days later, he called her and told her he was coming over. It was a Sunday, and she had hoped he would be there a few hours before her friends arrived. The few sparks of her passion for him remained—though the embers in the fire were much diminished.

Maybe they could rekindle the fire.

Maybe he would be sorry.

Maybe he had forgotten.

Maybe she could revive the embers.

He came, but after her friends had arrived, exuberant. He chatted with them. She ignored him, dismayed, disturbed, and on edge. She went to the kitchen to get some snacks. He followed her. When they were out of earshot of others, he revealed, "I wanted you to suffer and pine as much as I had. I wanted my revenge for the suffering you have put me through." It was his turn to make her realize the pangs of longing, of desire unfulfilled.

Even as the revelation surprised her, this was the moment of reckoning for her. The cord which had connected her to him snapped.

She was not sure what he had meant. She did not reply; she did not analyze, did not feel anger or animosity. Suddenly she did not care. This was the demise of their relationship, and she never looked back. She was sad for him.

Later that night, she wrote in her diary:

Sometimes a look, a word, a sentence, a phrase, a facial expression could attract us to another and make us fall in love, and at other times a look, a word, an exclamation, or even an explanation could spin us out of the bubble, out of love.

Years later, she realized that he was in a dark, dingy, unadventurous black hole from where he wanted to be extricated but was unable to express himself. The darkness had permeated through him, cutting him like a knife, pervading his surroundings. It was too late to help. He had withdrawn himself from the world.

The Power Struggle

When John, Sylvia's ex-husband, left, she had let him go easily. He had been delaying the divorce proceedings, the alimony payments, the lawyer's fees, dragging the years of togetherness. She was glad that the fictitious life she led was drawing to an end.

He was relieved she had not drained him of money.

She was relieved to be able to breathe freely.

She sold her suburban home in New Jersey with its spacious rooms, kissed her flowers goodbye, and bought herself a one-bedroom condominium on the 15th floor of a high-rise building in New York City.

She remembered how much she had wanted the mansion in New Jersey with its spacious rooms and sprawling lawns during the early days of her marriage—the joy, the exhilaration of starting life with John.

'Was she to blame?' She erased the thought as soon as it surfaced.

'Was it the greed of Wall Street with its ups and downs that had made him aggressive and angry with himself which he then projected onto her?'

'Was it just that his real self, so well camouflaged during the dating years, had found its way out like a serpent,

45

opening its hood chasing her, stinging at her. She had darted away from those bites, stinging him back in her own way, avoiding the poison he was emanating.'

At night when he used all the power, he had to subjugate her; she had begun to cringe and then revolt. She had wanted a lover who would be nice to her during the day. She would have loved him back with all the wonders she had held within her.

That night she wrote in her diary:

Women are turned off by rude men. Do not expect a woman to be nice to you in bed if you are not nice to her the rest of the time. It was not a wham, bam, thank you, ma'am, in marriages. The relationship could evolve if both partners were good to each other. It was as simple as that. There were no masters or servants in unions. There were only two people who respected each other, not superficially, but for their intrinsic worth and love would follow. Otherwise, just as quickly as love arose, hate could throttle it down.

A new life. A new beginning. She heaved a sigh of relief as she looked at the airy, breezy New York apartment. It was tastefully decorated by the previous owner who had left behind all the decorations. She was thankful. It would have taken her months to make this place livable. She liked the ready-to-move-in idea, especially when she was getting two for the price of one. Sylvia loved a good bargain, 'Maybe eventually she would remove some of the pictures and substitute them with 'Monet,' perhaps the cheaper version of the real one.'

She sold her Prius hybrid. She did not need a car in New York City, and it would be expensive to retain. She could walk down, take the train, or even walk to work. Apart from a nagging urge for a change of scenery from the picket fence, cause-of-envy suburban existence, the nearness to work fit into the practical realm.

As the city lights flickered and night fell on that sweltering summer day, she felt empowered. Her previous home in the suburbs of New Jersey had been a reminder of the life that was, the joys, the sorrows which followed—the wallpaper chipping away, akin to the years of torment chipping at her soul. She recalled the exhilaration she had felt as a young bride, thrilled by the manicured, organized greenery and the large beautiful stand-alone homes of the Garden State.

New York seemed an excuse to get far away from the life she had lived, from John's sudden caprice, his mood swings or maybe they were floating on the surface all along, and she had chosen to ignore them, only permitting her mind to the headier palatable feelings of being in love.

Her adulterous love affairs, which began as an escape from the baritones of her noisy marriage, had exploited her vulnerability. The giddy feeling of excitement, of eating the forbidden fruit, had landed her with a thud on the floor.

She had gotten up, brushed the stains off, moved into this new apartment. The sultry sea breeze with its aroma of salt caressed her. She felt a surge of joy and confidence as she breathed the salty air. A place of her own was exhilarating.

'No man,' she told herself. She wanted to understand herself. She wanted to stay by herself and get to know herself. As night fell, she felt her confidence ebb a little. She was alone in her apartment. An intruder could walk in; the frightening thought was immediately followed by her activating the alarm system.

Later that day, she wrote in her diary:

An intruder could walk in when there was a man in the house, and the man may not be able to do anything, maybe not even distract the intruder and would perhaps contemplate his own deflection from the scene. But something about the presence of another human being, even if it was a child, somehow provided a sense of security, perhaps not real from fear of intruders.

As she looked out of the window, the night sky suddenly lit up; the lightning made the entire sky appear white. The white sky, the howling, roaring winds, the gigantic trees swaying in a fulcrum were like scenes from a horror film. She witnessed the tussle between the wind and the trees, the trees resisting the rustling winds, the sea unforgiving and relentless as the sky thundered. She covered herself with a bedsheet, hid her head under it, her body in a fetal position, in an attempt to drown the noise and the fear.

The next morning there was calm. The winds had subsided. The earth seemed to stand still.

Sylvia woke up that morning, thankful for the calm. She wrote:

Even the Gods are irritated at times, humbling the arrogance of man. Man, with his superior intelligence, thinks he can conquer it all.

As she watched the calm after the storm and the world return to its usual pattern of normalcy, her eyes fell on the picture-perfect roses in her miniature garden. Her poetic mind indulged itself, and she continued writing:

Ode to the Rose

Oh, Rose,

Thy name is so beautiful

You bloom with such vigor

Your petals are so perfect.

Your smell is so sweet.

For all the senses, you are a treat.

As she did with some of her writings, she uploaded it onto Facebook and waited for the 'likes.' Not many were forthcoming. People placed more likes on pictures than write-ups for some reason—she decided, disheartened.

Women Conclave

That morning Sylvia decided to invite her girlfriends to her new home. She ordered an array of appetizers and dinner. Each of the friends brought some food with them. Somehow women always brought food to the girly get-togethers, especially those who liked to cook. Despite her busy schedule, Sylvia's best friend Miriam showed up as always. Gaiety, camaraderie, and sisterhood flooded the room. They ate and chatted away. Each had a unique story to tell. A few were divorced. One was happily married to a rich guy. A twinge of envy darkened the otherwise gleeful home, but it was soon forgotten, and the friend was forgiven for being rich and happy.

Another complained about how hard it was to raise kids. "Why do we have kids?" The question went around. Too many answers and opinions came forth.

Sylvia had no extraordinary opinion. One day she would have kids. It was a biological need.

"Really?" came another opinion. "I would rather travel, spend as I please than be tied down and become a heavyweight stay-at-home."

Fame and bags

"You can always get a tummy tuck and a breast lift if your breasts sag," someone said, "most actresses do."

"All these actresses, they're so pathetic. Look at poor Sallie; she's so thin and such a nervous wreck."

"I wouldn't feel sorry for her, she can buy a room full of designer bags, and I have to think twice, maybe ten times, to buy one," another begged to differ.

"Fame is a double-edged sword. When you fall, there is nobody to pick you up. People trample all over you. And when you are a nobody, nobody cares; people prod and probe and ridicule you. It is worse if you're famous and have no money." The once upon a time, actress muttered. She hated to be recognized.

Twenty years ago, she had compromised her body, her soul to bask in the limelight. The high had been addictive. She had ridden the wave like a shining star speeding across the horizon. As the laugh lines deepened on her face, the rounds to the dermatologist intensified. Eventually, the Botox and the facelift could not bring back her youthful looks. She was forgotten, and as the wrinkles stood out, melancholy set in. She hid from the camera and the film fraternity. Slowly the producers and directors whom she had made rich left her side. Her husband, a famous film producer, was in the midst of a pond full of fish. He could bait them easily, and they fell for the dreams he sold them, of great stardom, of wealth beyond imagination, of fame beyond comprehension.

"If I were to regain my youth, I would not wish fame on anyone. It didn't allow you to move freely, to do the things you want to do without the prying eyes of people unknown to you, and passing judgment on your behavior, smearing your character as if you were their property. Every fall hits you below the belt, and then you wish you were incognito."

Her beauty had faded, and with that fame, stealing her identity.

"I agree, I wouldn't care to be famous," the designer-purse-wanna-have jibed.

"I surely don't want to have the six-inch stilettos hurting my feet. The stilettos came with the territory, you know," another remarked.

For the first time, the designer-bag-wanna-have was glad she was not famous. Her feet didn't hurt every day. One day she would own the designer bag, the day her credit score wouldn't be as rotten as it was today.

"Darn, why are these bags so expensive? They are not even made of authentic leather; they call it faux leather!"

"Oh, that is just fake leather," another opined.

"Is that synthetic?" someone queried.

"Not sure," but they are made of cheaper materials. What is more, they are made in countries where labor laws are non-existent and laborers live in appalling conditions. Some brands employ children in their factories. We buy it for twenty times the price."

"What? Are you saying the bag costs less than $10 to make?" The designer-bag-wanna-have questioned but continued, "Darn, I don't think I care to be adorned by the designers."

"I don't want to adorn my shoulders with animal products and with animal hide," the animal lover and protector-activist added.

"The advertisers and brands play on the low self-esteem, we humans develop watching the perfectly pretty, rich, and famous people strutting their products on the television and billboards. It is almost as if the advertisers give people a shot at self-esteem. They destroy it first by bombarding us with pictures of people enjoying life, in some exotic land, happy with their bags and shoes, make us feel inadequate and unhappy about not having all that. Then they promise to enhance our happiness and self-esteem by making us wear their products. And the poor victims burn a hole in their credit cards, spend money they don't have, to buy things they don't need and lo and behold, their self-esteem is still at its bottom, especially when they see a pricier boot worn by their friend," she went on to opine.

Credit Cards

"It was the vacation of my dreams," the Greece returned one spoke with her thrilled shrill voice. She was intent on changing the topic. "Of course, now my credit cards are maxed out."

"Oh, no," said the financially savvy one. "Can you believe that you will be paying 18% or more over and above your actual expenses? That is a lot of money." She dragged 'a lot' to create an impact.

The immediate-need-to-gratify friend questioned. "How would I ever go on a vacation on my teacher's salary?

I make $40,000 a year, and I barely take home $1,500 per paycheck after Social Security, Medicare, unemployment, income taxes, and God knows what other taxes are taken off. And now they're threatening to take away our Social Security and Medicare or make dents in them as well," she lamented.

"Well, then you work an extra ten hours a month to pay for your vacation. But credit cards will eat away, not just your money but also your peace of mind."

"I am a cashier at the food mart when I'm not teaching or correcting papers. And I have two kids at home and no husband." Her husband had died in the Iraq war when she was pregnant with their second child. The room went silent. Sylvia got up and hugged the widow and kissed her on the forehead.

"Bravo!" Everyone rooted for this widowed, single parent, who worked extra hours annexed from her kids to give her family and herself a decent life.

Sylvia made a mental note to bring the resilience of these women to her diary. But that would be later. They chatted animatedly. It was past 11 pm. They had to get back home.

Hugging and waving goodbyes, they said. "Till we meet again."

"We should do this at least once a month." They agreed.

"*Au Revoir.*"

Each was glad that they had vented, found support understood more about the other and themselves a bit. And this became Sylvia's monthly ritual.

Miriam had remained silent.

That night Sylvia wrote in her diary:

Little do we realize that the conventional commonplace life is a boon—the quest for the extraordinary, our bane. Inundated by the success stories flashed at us, celebrity stories splashed all over the glossy magazines, and the media, most of us lesser mortals, walked on this earth in a state of dereliction.

She continued to write about the famous movie star who had vanished into murkiness.

He reached glitzy heights very few can.

He rose high and then fell hard.

He was adored and then pitied.

He stared at us from every billboard, and then he hid his face for many years.

He mesmerized us with his movies and songs and then disappeared into obscurity.

His work continues to haunt and entertain through posterity.

Love

Sylvia was unable to sleep that night. She stood near the window watching the full moon, illuminating the dark sky with silvery shimmer. Hours went by. Gradually dawn with all its magnificence enveloped the horizon with an orange hue. The moon stood still; its silver now reduced as it gazed at the sun kissing the earth. The expansive yellow gold of the sun brought with it the chirping of the blue jays and the swallows. Sylvia felt the warmth of the early morning sun.

It had been over a year since Neil and she had become lovers. The intoxication still prevailed. She eagerly waited for him, carefully manicured herself for him. She was a bird in flight, soaring with joy. He was her breath, her life. She needed to breathe the same air as him, and her heart was torn with anguish when he was not near her. Her eyes sparkled, and her heart danced when she was around him.

Her colleagues remarked about the glow on her face. "She bloomed," someone had said.

"She looked younger," another had complimented.

"You are so radiant," expressed another.

Love, she wrote, is an exclusive bubble, excludes everybody. An addiction we do not want to get out of. Two people inextricably bound together until the bubble bursts. A small needle can do the trick.

Love is joy.

Love is torment.

Love is longing.

Love is anguish.

Love is a sparkle in the eye.

Love is that special smile.

Love is that exclusive look.

Love is a song.

Love is a bird in flight, soaring.

Love is togetherness.

Love is an emotion that has tormented and given immense joy since time immemorial.

Love is the edifice of society.

Love is the edifice of marriage.

Love is or is not.

Love exists or does not.

Love has a way of bringing out the best in people. It is an adornment unmatched by any other in men and women. As she wrote this in her diary, she wondered at the irony of relationships going south, tripping, and falling off the cliff.

Love has been immortalized, yet the same love could vanish once life took over.

Many couples lived parallel lives, discontent. Some searched for excitement through a newfound love, sometimes only to find out that it too can turn sour and stale.

Love was an affirmation of our inner and outer beauty as reflected by the lover, and when that love transformed, it could be ugliness hurled by two opponents.

It was a Friday. Neil usually spent Fridays with his wife and kids. That was the evening when they were all home early. It was their evening out with a movie followed by dinner. Fridays were sacred to Neil.

A sting of envy cut through Sylvia—she imagined Neil's wife Sonia dressed impeccably, smiling at Neil as they sat opposite each other—Neil, warming up to his wife and serving the kids their favorite chicken burgers. She tried to distract herself from this discomforting chatter in her mind. She yearned to call Neil that day, feeling the need for reassurance—she longed to hear that he still loved her, that she was the one, that he craved for her just as much as she did, that this would last forever. Her last thought was agonizing.

'Forever! Would he ever leave his kids and wife for her? What was she thinking? Would she want him to?'

Sylvia wanted a family, kids, a soul mate. Neil was perhaps her soul mate, but the practicalities of their existence would not allow for anything further, and she was pragmatic enough to know that. Despondent, she stayed awake till the wee hours of the morning waiting for dawn to wake the rest of the world. She had no one to turn to. Her life was a secret, guarded from her friends, her family, and their prying eyes. She could not bear to be judged for loving a man—for loving Neil. The only person she could confide in was perhaps Neil. Even a shrink would say, "Breakup and move on." She decided to broach the subject of the future as if the present was not enough with Neil.

The Cup is Always Half-Empty

Why is the present never enough for mankind? Were we just tuned that way? Were our brains wired never to feel enough? Most philosophers wanted us to subjugate this feeling of inadequacy, that we were never enough, that something was amiss, and look at the cup as being half-full. Sure, philosophy brought peace, even if it lasted only a few minutes, or in some cases, hours, Sylvia pondered. This feeling of inadequacy was a pathetic sentiment. And yet, it was a robust force, which was the impetus to exceed our limits, our expectations.

The next day she finished her diary and waited for Neil. Neil rang the bell a few times. As she ran to open the door, happy, suddenly, the questions she had meant to ask him were driven away by his presence.

"God, I missed you, Sylvia." She heard the outpourings of a sincere heart.

"Last evening was a disaster. My daughter is growing into this rebellious creature. It is all my wife's influence. It is her fault. Sonia and I had a massive fight."

A massive heart attack was decipherable, but somehow, Sylvia could not comprehend this 'massive fight' as an adjective and noun. She could not imagine Neil, who was always kind and sweet to her, having a massive fight.

"You guys didn't hit each other, did you?"

"Almost," he replied. Sylvia could not help but wonder at the irony of her imaginary musings about the cohesiveness of his family and the reality of his life. She could not bring up her future when his present was so disturbed.

He grabbed her with a vengeance and planted his lips on hers, almost with a need to forget every misgiving in his life. He raised her skirt and came inside her. Had she loved him less, she may have resented this act.

Later she wrote:

Sex was not always the perfect synchronous culmination in the loins; both party's needs met, after which they rocked their heads on the pillows, with the smug smile of satisfaction on their lips. Sex was a man coming prematurely, a woman rarely getting an orgasm yet pleasured. An inability to perform well, a doubt whether the other enjoyed it. And sometimes just a culmination of the need in the loins. One could tolerate all these vagaries of sex only if the longing, the yearning for each other matched, and when the brain sent out love signals.

61

Love was this intangible sentiment that clothes sex and the family. And words mattered. Kind words could nourish the love plant.

Harsh words, comparisons, belittling could destroy this intangible love plant.

She called it the love plant she wrote because it needs constant nurturing, watering, and sunshine to prevent it from withering away.

For now, she would not think of her future, yet it kept gnawing at her. Somehow the future always seemed the most critical part of our present. Enjoy the moment, she told herself in vain.

She was glad Neil, and she had not had any screaming matches—this was a side of Neil she would not particularly respect or want to experience.

"You have to let children be. Let them succeed on their own terms and not yours, and they might surprise you," Sylvia advised.

"How do you know, you have none of your own," his frustration resounded, almost deafening her.

There was dead silence. She got up and walked to the kitchen, hiding the tear which was refusing to stay contained in her eyes. Neil had expected an outburst, a poisonous arrow flying towards him, and had braced himself for a war of words.

Her words had dried up—her mouth was parched. She could not bear this torment anymore. He entered the kitchen, poured himself a glass of water, gulped it as if to squelch his turmoil. Her back was toward him. She did not want him to see the hurt he had caused, or maybe the hurt circumstances had caused her. He gently held her arms and swerved her towards him. He saw the tears flowing from her cheeks—her sobs choked into silence to masquerade her agony.

He hugged her to his bosom hopelessly, helplessly—her tears soaking his shirt and chest. He held onto her and the moment, savoring every second. The salt of her tears felt sweet as he wrapped his arms around her tight as if it were to be the last time. He knew he had to let her go for her sake. It was a moment of reckoning. The future she had been so concerned about was staring her in the face. There would be no future with him. Their future, which he had been least concerned about and had taken for granted, would no longer belong to him. He would have to move away from her so that she could live the life she was meant to live. 'A good husband and six kids,' the thought brought a smile cutting through the sadness he felt. She would be a good mother and a good wife—he ruminated as he looked tenderly at her, his eyes numb and wet.

Men could cry too.

He would go back to his life of work, rearing kids, and even learn to tolerate his wife's indifference. Maybe that would be his life, but knowing Sylvia, loving her, and knowing that she loved him made everything tolerable. He did not call Sylvia that week. He suffered. The acute pain found release in angry retorts thrown at his wife and kids. Sylvia did not call him either. There were unspoken words that they both understood. Words and meanings conveyed through the tears, the eyes, and the tight hugs. Their hearts heavy, their minds determined, the tears were deliberately stopped in their path. A week later, the eyes were dry, but the lips remained parched. They went about their chores, working like robots.

Being a robot would be helpful. Get all the work done without the emotional cataclysms.

Wednesday evening, the evening Neil would come. That Wednesday, Sylvia was cognizant that he would not be there to fill her with rapturous love. There would be no conversations, no convulsive laughter, no forgetting the reality of their existence. The reality had arrived. He had gone back to his family, and she had made the conscious decision to move on. Her biological clock was ticking.

Depression And Anxiety

As the evening matured and the pink sky turned violet, and as darkness fell, Sylvia lay in bed watching the full moon move across the trees, playing hide and seek with the clouds, the gentle breeze rustling the leaves. Listening to the songs of the night insects attempting to attract their mates, she sighed as she contrasted her life when the phone rang. A multitude of emotions was doing the tango, flitting, and dancing, falling, and getting up, causing pain and fear making her teary-eyed.

She got up, butterflies churning in her stomach, ran to pick her cell phone with the expectation of hearing from the person she did not wish to hear from at the same time.

The Head and the Heart were constantly jabbing at each other. The heart usually rules the head, especially in matters of the heart.

Disappointment engulfed her as she saw the picture of her friend Rosie on the phone.

"I'm very depressed; I need to talk. Can I come over?"

Sylvia was feeling emotionally drained and in no mood to receive a visitor. Her life was at a crossroads, at a fork where she had to make choices or was Neil making choices for her?

"Yes, come," she replied hesitantly.

"Open the door." Sylvia was surprised to find Rosie at her doorstep as she disconnected the phone.

"I had to come. Otherwise, I would have killed myself." Her distraught, suicidal friend trembled as she spoke. Words came out of her mouth fast. "I am of no use to anyone. I think my husband and kids would be better off without me."

The deep darkness Rosie was swathed in was palpable.

Sylvia searched for words to comfort Rosie as she hugged her and bid her to sit. "Your children need their mother. No woman can love them more than you do. Your husband has provided for you, supported you all these years, and you want to leave him in the lurch now?"

Sylvia had not just been a spectator but a crutch in Rosie's life. Rosie had suffered from depression since her adolescence.

Somehow Rosie was absorbing Sylvia's words like a sponge. "I have done some nasty stuff." Sylvia waited to hear. Rosie spoke of her incestuous relationship at the age of thirteen.

"Well, if others have forgiven you, isn't it time you forgave yourself?" Sylvia's sensibility slowly seeped into Rosie. She had a listener in Sylvia, and that was all she had needed in this hour.

Sylvia went into the kitchen and returned with some hot chocolate for both of them. The sweet aroma of the chocolate drink drifted through the air. Sleep tugged at both of them.

After days of sleeplessness, our body has a way of snatching sleep out of us.

"Go and sleep on the bed. You are tired. Sylvia led Rosie into the bedroom and tucked her into the bed, gently rubbing her palm onto Rosie's forehead till she heard Rosie's rhythmic breathing as she slept.

Sylvia went back to the living room, sat on the sofa, wondering about depression. Was depression genetic? Sylvia remembered Rosie saying that both her parents had suffered from depression and worry. Once when Rosie was ten years old, her father had told her that 'if he died, he would want her to die with him. This world can be cruel to young girls.' Those words of death and fear had stuck with Rosie and Rosie, perpetually worried that her loved ones would die and that she would die with them. The first seeds of worry had been sown on the guileless mind of the child. Play and toys were a distraction, but anxiety became the constant companion in her head. Later she would host parties to be around people, to distract herself from her thoughts, but behind the smile and the greetings lurked the feeling of doom, a foreboding. She worried that her children would die and like her father had done before her, she would share this fear with her child. "I may not see you," she told her daughter as her daughter climbed the school bus and bade her goodbye. Unable to bear her overwrought mind, she had rushed to Sylvia's place. Sylvia had always given her a listening ear.

"My face is full of acne scars. You must hate to look at my face." Rosie had once queried. "I have always hated my skin. It is dry and coarse." She was preoccupied with self-hate.

Self-hate leads to low self-esteem.

Sylvia had smiled and answered with all sincerity. "I have not noticed your scars. I only see your beautiful smile and eager chuckle."

Many a time, we need someone else's approbation to understand ourselves and our self-worth. It is strange how we internalize our flaws to the extent that we take them to be true. We may even believe that everybody is perceiving, scrutinizing, and ruminating about our imperfections, that everybody is concerned with our weaknesses. The truth is, others see us from their perspective, good or bad. And most of these others are so preoccupied with their own lives that they really are unconcerned about us or anybody else.

"Rosie, just as I don't see the pain behind your smiles, I don't see the scars on your face."

"I know I can camouflage it very well. Nobody knows I am a depressed wreck ready to fall into a well and disappear into the ether. I am feeling sick."

Rosie was sick, not with the flu, but with the rattle and noise of her thoughts.

68

"You are a nice, charming woman who has a decent home, a supportive husband, and kids. Many men would have left if only to escape the stifling death-like air in a house filled with bleakness and gloominess."

Her husband, a family man, had stood by her and the kids, valuing the institution of marriage above his happiness.

Sylvia continued her diary:

Depression

It was genetic or biological triggered by some weird wiring of the brain and sometimes a response to events that happened to us.

Some people responded poorly, harming themselves in ways detrimental to their well-being while others flow with the current. Whether you swim or sink depends on how your brain is wired, your upbringing, your environment, but most importantly, how you react to the event. Do we then have the ability to overcome depression? There are many success stories of conquering depression, but not just by popping a pill. Contrary to popular belief, there were no quick-fix aids, but more through conscious effort, rewiring our brains, building our self-confidence, understanding the cliché, 'Life is what you make of it.' Most importantly, taking responsibility for our emotions. Being consciously aware of our thoughts is the first step and then slowly replacing them with better and more positive thoughts.

"Loving oneself is the first step to healing," Sylvia added.

"How can I love myself? I am ugly, a bad mother, a bad wife, and I could not even establish a career. I have left so many jobs because my mind strays a lot. I find it difficult to focus because of my demonic mind."

"Really! Are you a bad mother, a bad wife?" Sylvia questioned. "I don't see any ugliness or bad children in your house. You think it is so. Tame your straying mind. Go outdoors, run, soak the warm sun."

"It is cloudy, wet, and there's a storm outside." Rosie laughed. They both laughed. The air had eased. Rosie started to feel better. Sylvia opened a bottle of wine, and they slowly sipped and decided to enjoy the cloudy, damp, stormy night that they glimpsed through the window. It would be sunny tomorrow. For now, they made a mental note to take delight in the wet storm pitter-patter and form waves sinuous with the gusty speeding winds.

The rhythmic beauty of nature with all its litheness was stark. The tall trees with their large branches swayed in harmony with the winds. There was a moment of bewildering wonderment. Somehow, they felt alive. A flicker of peace settled in Rosie's heart.

Such moments of peace are what kept hope alive in humans.

Rosie smiled. This time there was no demon hiding in her head as she whistled and sang with joy. She would firmly resist in its path any wrong thought disturbing her. She would stop it from disquieting the peace she had found. She would stop envying anyone with better skin, which was perhaps everyone she met or knew. She would stop comparing the lady next door whose husband appeared more caring or the neighbor whose children were thriving.

Envy and comparison are the two unwarranted and untrue emotions that can kill peace.

You can never know the battles people are fighting in their minds.

Plato, the philosopher, had said eons ago: 'Be kind to everyone you meet for each is fighting a hard battle.'

They clinked their wine glasses. "To each his own," Rosie chirped.

"Cheers, Rosie."

"Thank you for being my friend, Sylvia. What would I have done without you? Maybe even killed myself. God opens doors."

When Sylvia did not know what to say, she smiled. This time she smiled and hugged her friend. Her sorrows had drowned, sunk to the bottom of the ocean after their *tête-à-tête*. "You have helped me too."

Curious Rosie wanted to hear more. "What, have you been depressed too?"

"No," Sylvia was emphatic. "No, I have not been clinically depressed, but I am suffering from a broken heart."

"Hope you find a new man who will mend your heart." Rosie guffawed naughtily as she got into the Uber and left.

It would take Rosie a few more years to overcome depression, but the seeds had sprouted, and the process had begun.

Peace in Silence

It was a new day, a new beginning. Neil was becoming a memory. A memory Sylvia was thankful for and would not lament the loss. "It was; it is not now," she told herself. "It could never have been permanent."

He had his baggage, the children, the wife, and he had plainly hinted that he did not want any more children.

"He was running out of steam raising the two he had," he had once remarked when she had casually mentioned children.

Neil was there when she had thought herself to be done with men. Decent men like Neil exist.

Men could love and still be vulnerable. The macho man seemed a myth. Maybe in physicality, but they were still assailable, she wrote.

Her life fell into a monotonous routine. She woke up, went to work, headed for the gym en-route to her single pad, where she came and dished out a small dinner of fresh vegetables, fish, and lentils, watched YouTube. On weekends she would have chores to get done, groceries bought, cooked—sometimes she indulged in dates with her girlfriends, only a few were single, most were married and raising children. Sylvia was beginning to get restless. She needed to find the right man, start a family.

Work was the distraction taking her away from the loneliness she was unable to get used to. Gradually the severe torture of solitariness subsided somewhat, giving way to acceptance of her circumstances.

Such is the fate of all pain when accepted. It dies away if allowed.

In this day and age, when the television blared from homes, people were on social media connecting, interacting, and reconnecting; Sylvia loved the silence of the twilight.

There was peace in silence. The twilight appeared like a red-gold necklace on the horizon. A flock of kites was flying home in synchrony. The colorful spring flowers adorning the gardens and homes seemed ready to receive the nightfall.

Sylvia rummaged through her laptop, looking for her daily teaching assignments at the university. The next day she was to give a lecture on social media at a seminar organized by a few corporations in collaboration with the university. Delegates from a few companies were expected to attend. Neil's organization was one of them.

Social Media

When she and Neil had decided to go their separate ways, Sylvia had taken a break from Facebook. She re-entered the life of social media cruising through the various posts she had missed. The pictures and scenery were a blur, as if seeing them through a speeding train. The blur did not stop her from clicking the like button on her friends' posts, and as she sped through them, none of the posts resonated with her. There were one too many bombarded every second. She had about three hundred friends or rather Facebook friends. The more friends one had on social media—the more was the clutter. How was one to cope with the chatting and the liking with a thousand friends, she mused. It surely would take hours out of one's productive time.

She heard herself speak. The microphone volume was loud, reverberating her soft voice through the auditorium of two hundred students, teachers, and administrators.

"Social media in every configuration is pervasive and has permeated all cultures universally. Its ubiquitous encroachment into the psyche of the young and the old is unambiguous. On the positive side connecting with faraway relatives and friends is easy. Social media is a great marketing tool to enhance your business and a great medium to exhibit your talents. Political movements have risen, and governments have fallen due to their impact. However, on the negative side, it was getting harder and harder to distinguish fabricated news from the real story. Reality itself appeared distorted. Dictators would interfere, thwart, and undermine democratic processes in sovereign lands.

Above all, the human psyche is undergoing an existential crisis. The carefully curated pictures abound with smiles. Every mundane venture seemed to take a life of its own. Somehow, going to restaurants, even if the food was insipid, appeared captivating in pictures, much to the envy of peers. Distant vacation destinations are showcased, almost as if to validate their lifestyle. Hugs and kisses between couples are picturized and posted unasked for even if, in actuality, the feelings are not genuine. Every aspect of life is on display.

The pretentious splendor is splashed all over. The number of 'likes' is counted anxiously. And if someone had failed to click the like button, it is considered a personal affront. Friends become enemies. Birthday parties and the like are promulgated much to the chagrin of the uninvited friends.

The human need for approbation is obliterated by this very public exposure of invincibility.

Social media on our phones is distracting, ruining our ability to concentrate on a task for more than a few seconds or minutes. We speak less with our friends and 'liked' more. We surely don't like them walking through exotic lands while we are at the desk, working away, listening to our boss's disapprobation.

What is then the anatomy of likes? Did we click the like button so that we could expect to receive the same, or is it to show a modicum of solidarity towards our friendships? Perhaps a bit of both, but more so the former for we humans as a race compared and contrasted our lives with each other.

Teenagers take down their pictures if the number of 'likes' they receive is perceived to be inadequate. Random strangers are hired to 'like' a photo to give a semblance of popularity.

'Comparison is the thief of Joy' was so rightfully noted by President Roosevelt decades ago, and social media made it easier for friends to be pitted against each other.

We shield ourselves from exposing our inner trepidation, even to our loved ones. We keep our sadness to ourselves, suppressing our words before they can be vocalized. How could we not when everybody else seems so perfect?

Expressing our vulnerable side creates deeper friendships.

Our support system is dwindling, depression is on the rise, and creativity is getting smothered. This generation is too busy liking, commenting, comparing, competing, and many a time envying. The mind has no room to process any other vocation. Social media is becoming a platform for vanity validation. Narcissism, with its associated insecurity, is spreading. Most activities on social media are self-obsessed. Children in their formative years and adults are getting addicted; the slight endorphin release on seeing a new text or message or a complimentary comment is soon followed by an emotional crash.

Social media is a platform where we can voice our opinions without any hindrance or resistance. It can help satisfy a whimsical part of ourselves, but is that good for us?

Social media is bringing us closer yet alienating us.

Television, on the other hand, with its make-believe, fantasy, had the ability to numb people's sense and sensibility.

People watched the television when they were bored and mostly when they returned home from work. The constant media bombardment of larger-than-life images, flashy clothes, fancy shoes, jewelry, and mansions were on the television because people devoured them. Yet, the viewers were left with a feeling of inadequacy in comparison. The reality of their existence never living up to the images thrust upon them. Somewhere television was changing our culture.

Happiness was equated with money. The two may complement each other but were not dependent on each other. Understand the difference.

Television was in every home, and the lifestyle touted on the idiot box was influencing the psychological well-being of humans, especially children in their formative years. The size four women in the soap-operas appeared confident and seemed to know exactly what to do or say, unlike the rest of humanity. The news was a noisy, confusing opinionated drama. The advertisers had amassed great wealth through the propagation of colas to sweet savories, beers, cigarettes, and the like, each of them detrimental to the health of the consumer. The baby boomers had lapped up these endorsements, and as a consequence of which, obesity, diabetes, high blood pressure, and cancers had multiplied.

Sure, there were other reasons for diseases to surface and manifest.

On the positive side, television has a lot of educational content, valuable information on current affairs, entertainment, and artistically created dramas, voraciously consume these, she added. And please enjoy those late-night comedies and one of my favorites, The Oprah Show.

Thank you all for listening, and if we can limit our media time, my lecture would have served its purpose," she said as she ended the talk.

Sylvia did not hear the thunderous applause. A man was walking towards her, who had the effect of stunning her brain. He was clapping his hands as he walked towards her to take the microphone.

"Ladies and gentlemen, I do think this lady has eloquently dealt with this modern and not so modern devil slowly creeping into our lives," he concluded. The crowd cheered. This time Sylvia heard the applause. Neil held her arm and walked her from the stage. She did not look at him.

There was an after-party arranged for all the organizers and the speakers. He took her to a table where the appetizers and the drinks were kept.

Pouring himself a glass of wine, he said, "I miss you."

She did not reply. He was waiting for an answer. "I love you," he added, not consciously aware of the surroundings he was in. She nudged him to stop, painfully aware of the surroundings they were in.

Exasperated, she moved away from him with the pretext of meeting other acquaintances. His eyes searched across the room for her, but she had vanished.

Divorce

Neil went home dejected that night. His wife was watching the television. She heard his footsteps but did not look up to greet him.

"Hi," he said as he walked up the stairs to his bedroom feeling emotionally fatigued.

"I want a divorce," he heard her scream.

Suddenly the chill in the air became apparent. "Why?" Neil asked despite himself.

"You are asking me why when you're cheating on me."

'Cheating on me,' the phrase hit him hard. He didn't feel he had cheated. He had loved, and he had felt alive. The word demeaned him, demeaned everything he stood for. Somewhere he had sought love and had received it, but outside his marriage. He felt irked. He was about to say I'm not cheating on you—instead, he asked. "What makes you think so?"

"Your ex-secretary called me." She was at the after-party.

Word had gotten around fast.

He knew he had acted stupidly that evening. He had missed Sylvia. When he had seen her after all these months, he had forgotten all about restraint.

"I'm going to sleep."

"Sleep, I need answers. How long has this been going on?"

"Sonia, there is nothing between us."

"Stop lying, and she's not even beautiful."

His ears perked up. Astounded, he wondered how that was even relevant. He found Sylvia incredibly attractive. A smile escaped his lips.

"You're smiling. Is this a joke? You will hear from the divorce lawyer tomorrow, and I will take every penny away from you." Her vengeance increased in proportion to his smile.

"I'm not having an affair." He replied truthfully. I am with you and the children."

"So, you are with me for the sake of the children?"

"We will talk tomorrow." He went up to his bedroom and slammed the door shut.

Her rage knew no limits. Her heart was pounding— she felt a stabbing pain in her stomach. She had to reach out to someone. Her ego would not allow her to knock on Neil's room. She called her friend. As she spoke, her pain eased. She rattled the story of her husband's affair.

"Leave him," came the prompt advice. The feminist wave was rampant.

Crisis Meeting

The next day Sonia's friend called a crisis meeting. Seven friends showed up.

"Leave him for God's sake," commented one."

"Don't take this lying down," came another opinion.

"I would have left him, what a creep," lashed another.

"I did not expect Neil of all men to do this. He seems such a family man," a fourth comment was hurled.

"All those Facebook pictures you posted of Neil, and you were such a sham," came the fifth comment stated with a sense of victory.

Sonia heard the first four comments with zest. They vilified Neil and reinforced her decision to leave.

The Facebook-picture-comment infuriated her.

Her eyes glared at this villain, "How dare you call my Facebook pictures a sham? They were genuine when I posted them."

No one had any clarity as to what Sonia was trying to say. She had posted them a month ago.

The sixth lady trying to break the unease and wanting to appear on the side of Sonia and hence feminism, explained: "Theirs was an envious marriage till this slut came into their lives. Men will be men—they always fall for sluts," she said, thinking of her husband's philandering ways. She had tolerated her husband for the sake of her children, for the family unit, and because he was a great provider. Her escape from this affliction was to shop. She spent all her energy buying diamonds. She had a private jeweler who custom-made the latest and the most exquisite cutting-edge pendants and necklaces. He had taught her to distinguish the cheap from the expensive to the most valuable diamonds. She trusted her jeweler more than her husband. He would never cheat her—he sold them to her at a fair price; so, she thought with satisfaction. She would wear a different set for every party. No one envied her. They understood her and felt sorry for her.

Some people found an anchor in diamonds, some in demigods, some with alcohol, and many other ways. Each was crying to fulfill a depleted part of their soul.

They were eagerly waiting for the last comment. It was thoughtfully articulated with some reservation—the last speaker was apprehensive of becoming a pariah, the only one in the party with a different point of view. She felt compelled to say. "Give your marriage a chance; talk to Neil. Both of you should get some counseling from an unbiased third person."

"Do you understand that he just battered and bruised me? I have some self-respect." Sonia's voice was loud as it reverberated through the house.

"You have children together," the pariah answered.

"He doesn't deserve them. I will see to it that they hate him just as much as I do."

Pariah: "That would not be good for the children—it would be a disservice to them."

Battered one: "Well, he should have thought of that when he went around sleeping with a gold digger. And she's not even pretty."

"Have you seen her?" bellowed the first one.

The second one: "I can't believe he would want someone ugly when he has a pretty wife at home."

The third one: "Beauty lies in the eyes of the beholder," she repeated the age-old soothsaying with conviction.

Sonia felt compelled to interject. "I was the beauty queen of my class."

The Fat Lady

Fourth one: "Me too, I was wafer-thin then, and now I have put on so much weight. I hate myself and what I have become. My husband keeps calling me 'fatso.' He says he is not turned on by me because of my weight, worse—he won't allow me to eat the desserts I crave so much."

I detest myself all the more when I see my classmates looking so thin and happy," she drawled almost as if she had prepared the speech for many months and was waiting for the right moment to ventilate.

The fifth one: "I'm fat too, but my husband dotes on me. We care for each other. My weight doesn't seem to bother him. He has a potbelly too, is balding, and I couldn't care less."

The fourth one was now glum, feeling even more wretched.

Sonia was getting impatient. The conversation was not revolving around her as she had hoped. "You know men still make passes at me. I have a colleague at work who always calls me beautiful. We chat a lot. He finds me remarkably interesting."

"Does Neil know?"

"Of course not. There's nothing serious, and if I were to tell Neil, it would upset him."

The intellectual pariah added. "It is better that way. You cannot tell your husband everything. They will just put two and two together and make eight. You know what I mean. Are you attracted to him?"

"No," replied Sonia. "He's not very good-looking. I like the way he distracts me from work, especially the times I need or feel stressed. I think he is in love with me, though. He did tell me that once, but I ignore that aspect. It is flattering to see the pine in his eyes."

"You mean he pines for you?"

"Yes," Sonia claimed. Somehow the thought of the office distractor calmed Sonia a bit.

The intellectual pariah: "Sometimes it is good to have such distractors. It takes your mind off the mundane and even better if you're not in love with him, but you know that he is. I agree it is flattering as we age with no price tags attached to it."

85

The Platonic Affair

The fifth one: "I was in grad school, in my late thirties, married with kids; I had a crush on this professor who was twenty-two years my senior. He was a tall, slender, athletic, light-skinned man with light hair who would stare at my face with admiration. One day he threw flying kisses at me. I pretended not to notice them. I was going through a very rough patch. My supervisor and I were at loggerheads. I was afraid of being thrown out of school.

A few days later, I went straight to this professor's office and told him about my fears. "You are a wonderful person. Those people are going to drive you crazy." He spat those angry words at my supervisor."

His words helped. His belief in me helped. I dreamt of him hugging and kissing me, but that never happened. I would dress impeccably and deliberately cross his path in school. He would look up and smile. It would brighten my day, and at night, I would drift off thinking of him kissing me, and these thoughts helped me sleep. This platonic love affair went on for a year, and somehow, I was able to handle one of the worst periods of my career stoically. I graduated. After the ceremony, I went to his office and met him. Restraining a tear, I told him that I was fond of him. He held my hand across the table and said the feelings were mutual. I left school and never met him again. Of course, I didn't tell my husband, but it was also a period that brought me closer to my husband. For the first time in seventeen years, I had seen this new side of the man I had married. He supported me, advised me, restrained me while the supervisor was badgering me with a vengeance trying his best to destroy my career. I fell in love with my husband of 17 years all over again."

"Why did the supervisor try to destroy your career?" asked the pariah.

"I think he was trying to build a name for himself and justify his position as someone who weeded the weaker candidates. I was not a weak candidate, but I had kids, and when others in my class partied, I would rush back to my kids. He sensed I was the odd man, or rather woman on the team, and felt I would be an easy target with not much support from the rest of my classmates with whom I was not socializing anyway. He was short, stocky with little knowledge of the subject, insecure, and when he rose to power, he used it to hide his feelings of inferiority."

Sonia was agitated. "He wants an ugly duckling over me. So be it."

Her ego bruised, hurt; she hated Neil for doing this to her, for making her the laughingstock among her friends. She had portrayed a curated picture of life with him, the large house, the luxurious vacations. She had carefully managed to hide the emptiness she felt by ignoring it. Now her carefully guarded secret was out on display for everyone to ridicule. Her love for Neil had dwindled over the years. Through the years of raising her kids and focusing on her career, she had been oblivious of him most of the time, except at parties where he was the trophy she showed off, on vacations where she looked into his eyes or held his arms as the pictures were being clicked.

Sonia felt her world collapse. "What would the world think?"

"You are not a famous person that the rest of the world has to worry about you," the socialite retorted. She had gone through her very own public humiliation.

87

"I don't think you should worry about others and what they think. What is that you want?" The intellectual one queried.

"I want to take his money, the kids, and leave him penniless."

"Of course, you should leave him," came a synchronous loud chant from the other six friends.

"It's not easy, but we will be there for you."

"It's time to leave; it is getting late." The intellectual friend was deliberately ironic.

Her decision endorsed by the majority—Sonia hugged her friends one by one and bid them goodbye. She walked into her bedroom, depleted—her mind wrestled between needing a shuteye and feeling animated by anger. She must have slept for an hour when the clinking of the teapot in the kitchen woke her. She lay in bed, hoping for sleep to numb her. 'Why was this happening to her?'

'The gnawing emptiness of all the yesterdays seemed a million times better than the hollowness of today.'

A tornado churned inside her. Lying in bed was torturous. She decided to get up and go to work.

To be gainfully employed is a blessing. It does not just give us our identity, but somewhere, it can take our minds away from the searing pain.

She went downstairs to the kitchen. Neil was getting breakfast ready. "Tea," he said with an expression close to a half-smile, unsure whether to smile or stay glum when he felt her presence. She did not reply.

"Tea," he asked again.

"No." Her voice was loud and emphatic.

"Let me make you some tea. Why don't you sit, and we can talk?"

"Neil, is there anything to talk about? You have crossed the line."

"Sonia, I'm not having an affair."

"Oh, so you have broken up with her."

"Yes."

"But you were professing love to her yesterday."

"It was a mistake."

"What was, professing love or getting caught?"

"Sonia," he reached towards her. She shoved him away.

"Sonia, we have grown apart."

"Oh, so now we can be together after what you have done."

"I'm sorry."

"Sorry for what, Neil?"

"Sorry for hurting you."

"But you're not sorry about the affair, about your love for her?"

He looked at his feet. He did not have a reply.

"I cannot live with someone I cannot trust."

"I promise not to hurt you again, Sonia."

She looked at him, her eyes sad, wishing he would hold her and say it was all a lie, that she was the only woman who had rocked his heart. He would never say that—never feel that. She knew he had not loved her in some years. He had surely cared for her and the kids. He got up and hugged her. There was no passion, no love. There was no warmth in her reciprocation, either. Maybe it was time for them to separate even if there was no third person, she speculated.

Sonia was pensive. "I cannot forgive you."

"I will not see her again," Neil pleaded as if taking an oath. He knew that to be a lie.

"Don't lie to me any more than you have; you like that slut."

Neil struggled to control his anger. 'How dare you' were his first thoughts; he bit his tongue instead.

"A man like you doesn't deserve me. I can find ten others who would rave over me."

"Why don't you?"

"So, this is what you want. I have been faithful to you despite all those men wooing me at work." He was a bit taken aback. He had never felt insecure, and the thought that other men would woo a forty-year-old woman had not crossed his mind. He thought of Sylvia; she was thirty-five, well, almost forty. His reverie was interrupted.

"I'm filing for divorce. You will pay me every penny you earn. I'm keeping the kids. You are irresponsible, and I don't want them to be influenced by a man like you," she said, venom flowing through her mind and veins, directionless.

"Calm down, Sonia. I am not going anywhere. They are my kids too."

"You have never been there for them between work and your affair, no wonder you were late every night." Suddenly her lonely nights flashed in front of her making her want to scream.

"We need to talk. Sit down." Neil's aggressive voice irked her, but she found herself reluctantly obeying him, hoping for that one straw of redemption.

"The affair is over. Let us go for counseling. Let us iron out things between us. We are a family unit."

"Oh, so when you were in bed with her, you must have cared a lot about the family unit. I am sure you were thinking of the kids and me." Her taunt was acidic.

Sonia's mother was on the phone, coaxing her to go for counseling. "Neil is a good boy. You must give him a chance. It is not easy for a woman to stay alone and raise kids without a man. He's a good provider too and has always respected me."

"Okay, so he respects you, and that makes him a good boy."

"I want you to stay married, my child. I think you should go to counseling."

Counseling

A few days later, the counselor was confronting them. She asked them about their childhood and how they had met.

"He pursued me."

"Yes," he agreed. "Sonia was the most beautiful girl I had met."

Counselor: "Were you in love with each other?"

"Hopelessly," he said, his eyes smiling at the memory.

Sonia looked at Neil quizzically, wondering where it had all disappeared. "I loved him too."

Counselor: "Then what happened?"

"Our sex life is not compatible," Neil spoke softly, not wanting to sound offensive.

Sonia: "What, he is lying. We have sex once or twice a week."

Counselor: "Who initiates it, most of the time?"

They were quiet. Somehow discussing their intimate reality even to a professional counselor seemed embarrassing.

Counselor: "There is a difference between having sex and enjoying sex."

The silence continued.

Counselor: "What are some of your common interests?"

They looked at each other unable to think of anything other than their children.

Sonia was getting exasperated. "What has this got to do with Neil's infidelity?"

Counselor: "Infidelity need not be a reason to annul a marriage."

"The courts don't seem to think so. My friend is a lawyer, and she said I could fleece him for this."

Counselor: "Sonia, let me explain. I don't want you to get to the courts. I want you guys to give each other a chance. If not for yourself, then for the sake of your children."

Sonia relented. "He can have them half the time."

Counselor: "Sonia, men and women stray sometimes. Perhaps they're not happy in their marriage, and maybe they are lonely. Give him a chance—give yourself a chance. Maybe you can bring the spark back into your lives."

"Damn, I should never have come here. Are you saying I'm the reason for his adultery?"

Counselor: "No, no, I meant that he might have strayed to find himself, to know more about himself. He may have strayed because a forbidden fruit is sometimes more intriguing."

Neil remained silent through all this. He had strayed because Sylvia and he had a similar wavelength and understanding; they had enjoyed each other's company, and they were physically compatible.

As he was thinking about the other reasons as to why he might have strayed, he heard the counselor say: "Your time is up. Please come back next week. Meanwhile, be nice to each other and say one good thing about the other every day and bring me a copy of all the niceties."

Sonia fumed as they got into the car. "I am never going back to her. You are a mean, irresponsible man, selfish to the core. Before having an affair, you could have at the very least thought of your children."

He racked his brain to find something complimentary about Sonia. Nothing came to his mind.

"I am sorry, Sonia. You don't deserve a mean-spirited guy like me." The mean arrow had left the bow, and he could not take the words back.

His sarcasm stung her.

"I absolutely agree. You are mean. Get out of my life."

His ego was knocked out of slumber. "Fine, if that is what you want." He did not want to take sole responsibility for the dissolution of their marriage. It was she who wanted it, and he was giving it to her. It was her decision.

Somehow it is easier for us if the decision is made by another. At least we need not worry about the repercussions of the decision if it turns out to be a mistake.

As they entered the house, they heard the phone ring. Neil answered the phone. It was Sonia's mother. "My child, how was the counseling?" she asked anxiously.

"It went well."

"Who is that? Is that your lover?"

"It is your mother, for God's sake," he yelled, covering the mouthpiece. "Here," he handed the phone to Sonia.

"Mama, I am tired." Sonia wanted nothing to do with anyone at that moment.

"When is the next counseling session?" Her mother's voice sounded worried.

"Next week, but I am not going."

"Please go, my child. Just go for my sake if you care for me." Her mother kept the phone down, sobbing as a foreboding ripped through her.

Parents go through pain when their children suffer.

Hesitantly, Sonia went for the next session. Neil had given up hope. The fights, the taunts were leaving him bereft of sleep and sanity.

"We don't have any paper saying cordial things about each other," he remarked as he resignedly sat on the couch next to his wife.

Counselor: "Let me explain. Some couples learn to forget the past, are able to forgive, and can find happiness with each other, but one has to forgive and forget and not broach the subject of straying again and again. Can you let bygones be bygones and start anew? You may be the lucky couple who can strengthen the marriage better than it was. You would give a second chance to someone else, wouldn't you? Why don't you give yourselves a second chance?"

"Ma'am, why don't you understand? He is an irresponsible miser. He has never bought me a gift, not even artificial jewelry worth a few dollars."

Neil was not sure whether to reply. "If I buy something, she doesn't approve of it; hence, I have stopped buying anything for her. I let her do the shopping." He let his mind do the talking.

"See, see, I'm right. I work, I shop, I take care of the house while he philanders away."

Counselor: "The need to be right is so ingrained in us humans. Sometimes or rather, many a time, it is okay to let the other person be right. More harm is caused by wanting to be 'right' than otherwise."

Neil muttered, "So true. It was true among friends, among colleagues too."

He was impressed by the counselor's insight.

"For crying out loud, if I am right, he should learn to apologize. Can men not apologize?"

"Ma'am, sorry and apology are the same, aren't they?" Neil spoke with a smirk on his face.

"Wipe that sneer off. You are going to pay for this." Sonia screamed as she walked out.

"Sorry for wasting your time, ma'am. Can I get the bill for the sessions?"

"Neil, I will mail you the bill. Good luck. Sometimes people cannot look beyond their nose," she said apologetically.

Neil hoped for a discount. After all, Sonia had romped out halfway through the session, and both the sessions had been a disaster. Perhaps, the only conclusion which came out of the meetings was that it made him more than determined to get out of the marriage. It just did not seem right to stay with someone so rigid, who refused to relent even a little. He felt relieved once the decision was made.

Somewhere we are not only capable of drowning our partner's best but also bringing out the worst.

Ironically, he was leaving his wife at the same time as his lover was deciding to get married.

He had just received Sylvia's text. 'Hey, there is some good news. My parents had arranged for me to meet this guy. His name is Mark. We met a few times. I like him. I think he is the one for me. Maybe getting married soon.'

Neil was not sure if Sylvia was rushing into the marriage because her biological clock was ticking away or because she was lonely. Either way, it was something he had wanted for her.

'Congrats.' He texted her back, feeling acutely lonely.

He did not hire a divorce lawyer. He had no energy or inclination to fight any more battles. He was confronting a caged, hungry lion. He could have fought and perhaps alienated his kids. He would rather have his kids than the money. He decided to keep just enough for his sustenance and give the rest for his children's education and upbringing. In exchange, he would have his kids a few times a week and on weekends if they were not busy.

97

A few weeks later, Sylvia called him. "I am pleased, Neil."

It astounded him that she had found happiness so soon after they had split. It just didn't seem fair when he was trying to make sense of his life and the trajectory it had taken.

"I know it seems too soon." She could read his mind remotely. "I like him. He has a great sense of humor, and he likes me. He's a bit miserly, though. Doesn't buy me lunches when we go out, and he expects me to pay for mine."

"Money and sex are the two things that wreck marriages," Neil warned.

"Come on, Neil. I make more money anyway. I will not allow money to come between us. He gets a bit rude sometimes, but when I ask him to stop, he does. He is not egotistical and doesn't feel bad about listening to me. I think we will be fine."

Neil was surprised that Sylvia had noted these flaws during the early days of her courtship with Mark.

The courtships were times when we projected only our congenial side to people and also when we ignored the flaws of the other. That is how we tricked ourselves into marrying the 'perfect' man or woman.

"A courtship made in heaven leading to a marriage made in hell," Neil sighed. "Sylvia, I am happy you are realistic. Does this mean we will never see each other or talk to each other?" He was anxious to know.

"Don't be silly. Mark is not the kind of person who would feel insecure. We sure can talk, meet, but no sex." She had drawn the line.

"I am going through a divorce. Sonia and I are separating. I will buy a house close to hers so I can be with the kids every so often."

"What happened?"

Neil did not feel the need to tell that Sonia had known about them. "You know we have been incompatible."

"Thank God, it is not because of us. I would be extremely sad if it were. Reach out to me, my dear, if you need anything."

"Yes, I will."

'I need sex, I need you and want to be with you,' he thought but had no courage to vocalize. She seemed to have flown far away.

Sylvia felt a twinge of sorrow. Knowing Neil was alone was not a happy thought. Her optimism got the better of her. "You will find someone, and it will all be fine," she said half-heartedly.

"Are you planning to marry this dude despite all the flaws you have enumerated to me?"

"Isn't it better to get into a relationship knowing all the flaws of your partner than being blinded by the giddiness of romantic love?"

"If you are expecting to change him, it is probable, but most likely not possible. We do come with our permanent and not so permanent inner quirks." Neil cautioned.

"I do not intend to change him. I am willing to accept him as he is. Relationships thrive when we accept each other."

"Good luck, Madam relationship Guru! Good luck marrying Bark. The name reminds me of a dog."

Sylvia sensed a mean streak in Neil, something she had not noticed before, and was unpleasantly surprised. "Sounds like you are jealous, and his name is Mark."

"What kind of name is that? Is he taller than me?"

"Neil, why does it matter if he is taller or shorter than you. I do not compare the two of you."

"Let me know how he is in bed."

"For God's sake, Neil, you are behaving like a child. No, children are better—you are talking like a frustrated jealous man. I did not expect this of you."

"What were you expecting, Sylvia? Sanity, when my life is in shambles, and you seem to have got it all together."

She remained silent. All she wanted was to hang up and run, run away from this new Neil, this stranger Neil.

After a few moments of awkwardness, Neil apologized.

"I am sorry, so sorry, Sylvia. I shouldn't have spoken like this. I have no clue what got the better of me. It must be jealousy."

"Apology accepted, my dear Neil. Get some sleep. Sleep is always restorative. Goodnight."

Sylvia lay in bed, sapped after her conversation with Neil. A shade of Neil she had not suspected when they were together. Perhaps we were all weird at times—we all had our quirks. She wondered if she had any. She could think of none.

It was easier to see quirks and weirdness in others than in oneself.

That night Sylvia wrote:

Heroes and heroines exist only in the movies. They were beautiful, brave, bold, loving, caring, and sane all the time.

We humans, not on the celluloid, were kind, mean, rude, polite, gloomy, cheerful, changing our characters like the chameleon—yet our movies, our books taught us to expect that one perfect man or that one perfect woman and they said life would be one perfect rhythm.

Sylvia's mother had always told her, "No expectations, no disappointments."

We expect a lot, a lot from ourselves, from our partners, from our children, from our colleagues, from our bosses, and who in the world could live up to our expectations when we ourselves were flawed? Surprisingly, we could easily see the flaws in others, but somehow, we were blinded to our own flaws.

We want everyone else to change but ourselves.

"Change yourself, and the world will change." Her mother's words echoed in her ears.

A slight change in perspective could change the trajectory of relationships, she concluded.

The Immigrant Experience

As Sylvia concluded her diary for the day, her eyes fell on a picture of Seema in a local newspaper. Seema was her close friend from India. Young Seema was a pretty girl. A man had noticed Seema at a festival, proposed to her parents, asking for their daughter's hand in marriage. Seema's middle-class parents had been thrilled beyond reason. The girl had weighed on them like a ton of bricks. They had penny-pinched through the years, accumulated the outlawed dowry for her marriage, but it never seemed enough. Her marriage had been a point of contention between her parents. When this well-settled, handsome Indian-born, American suitor had proposed, their hearts felt light for the first time since her birth.

Seema had recently broken off with her boyfriend, who had refused to marry her. His parents had advised him to marry a rich girl, so he would not have to struggle much in life. A rich girl who could give him a car and a house in exchange for the stable government job he held.

Seema's parents decided that Seema would marry the American suitor. Seema did not object. She agreed to the arranged marriage. The wedding date was fixed. It would take place in 2 weeks. The American had flown to India for three weeks. That was all the leave he had. It was hard to prolong his stay in India. The company he worked for would not allow him extended time off. Seema felt no inclination to take part in making arrangements for her upcoming wedding. She detested her parents for being middle class. Her boyfriend had deserted her and had robbed her of the little self-esteem she had.

Here was this savior who had come from the first world, smitten by her beauty, had wanted to marry her, and had rejected any form of dowry in exchange. A momentary sense of elation swept through her. She could snub her ex-boyfriend—now that she had a suitor who would whisk her off to the first world. It elevated her status. Marrying someone from the first world was the ultimate dream of many parents with marriageable daughters. It was the ticket to a better life, a more prosperous life even though it meant transplanting the flower to an unfamiliar environment, a new culture. On her wedding day for the first time, Seema felt torn away from the thread, which had bonded her with her parents in love and sorrow, richness, and poverty. Her mother had sobbed relentlessly during the wedding, already missing her intensely, painfully aware that she may not see her precious daughter for some years. As Seema boarded the plane, thanks to the American tourist visa she had obtained a year ago, she too acutely missed her parents. She remembered her brother teasing her—his naughtiness had irked her then; it brought a smile now as she smothered her tears, wondering when she would see him again. She had no answers. It was expensive to fly back and forth. Seema was pensive throughout the flight. Her husband, a stranger, snored in the seat next to hers.

Mumbai

Seema's mind raced through the hustle and bustle of the city she had left behind. Mumbai, with its luxurious skyscrapers, juxtaposed against the appalling shanties. Noises of all kinds could be heard, from construction workers hammering away to the honks emanating from the vehicles on the road—the streets and the footpaths of the city teeming with people. The heat captured by the cemented brick walls of the buildings suffocating yet vibrant. The warm sea breeze, cutting through the humid mushy air, blowing away the pollution and the chemicals spurting out from the chimneys of unrestrained factories—numbing the smell of the sewers around which slums were built.

New Jersey

As she landed at Newark airport in New Jersey, the cold November wind stirred her. She shivered from the chill in the air. Her husband had kept an extra coat in his carry-on bag and handed it to her. As the car sped through the wide roads, an aloofness was palpable—the speeding vehicles an acknowledgment of a fast-paced lifestyle. The warmth of her homeland seemed non-existent here.

She entered her large home, looking around for some familiarity. The five-bedroom house with a front and backyard seemed like a castle compared to the small one-bedroom apartment in Mumbai, where she had lived with her parents, grandmother, and brother. Her granny and brother had slept on the kitchen floor—she had slept on the floor of the living room.

At 5 am when her father left for work, the whole household would be up, folding the foldable mattresses and bedsheets and placing them on the only bed they had, which belonged to their parents. She thought of the whizzing ceiling fan circulating the warm air, the heat from the roof drying her skin.

Her husband showed her the rooms. There was a living room, a family room, a large kitchen, a few bathrooms. She wondered if anybody else was staying with them. "Who is going to sleep here?" she asked, looking at the smallest bedroom in the house.

"That is the guest bedroom." This was a new concept for her. "This is our home, your home—occasionally, my mother will come and live with us. She is at my sister's place right now. I'm going to order some bagels and pizza for you." Seema had never heard of bagels, but not wanting to appear ignorant, agreed to what he had decided to order. They ate in silence. The silence in the house was not able to still her.

She missed the constant stimulation of the city she had left behind. She thought of her mother, who would be serving her with delicacies and fried snacks at this time, the steaming hot rice cakes and chutney. The aroma of food whiffing through the air of the small house, she had called home all these twenty years of her life, where she had laughed, fought, cried, got her way, impatient at the repetitive stories her granny told her. Her heart yearned for those stories now, feeling remorse at her meanness towards her family and her unruly behavior towards them in an urgent need to get her way.

She had been a shy child clinging to her mother's sari. She reminisced about playing and dancing in the rain, making paper boats and setting them afloat in the small puddles created by the raindrops during the monsoon season, avoiding the jumping frogs and the toads in tow.

Seema's thoughts drifted back to the long train journeys from Mumbai city to her village in the South of India every year to meet her mother's parents, who had lived there all their life. They had never wanted to stay elsewhere—their roots were entrenched in its soil. Eating goodies and snacks at the train stations—daydreaming as the train sped through the mountains and the plains—ecstatic, as the train cruised through the magnificent Vindhya mountains and the Western Ghats, bewitched by flora and fauna, and the waterfalls in the backdrop; waiting for the train to pass through tunnels in the mid-afternoon and squealing with joy as darkness fell on the compartments, and the train hooted through the valleys puffing off steam, thrilled to see the tail-end of the long train as it curved around the mountains. Vendors would climb aboard the train as the train slowed at the stations, in a frenzied effort to sell hot tea and mouth-watering snacks, stealthily moving from one compartment to the next as the savories were bought and relished. The homemade packed food made by her mother was shared with fellow passengers. She would soon learn that sharing food during mealtimes was a very eastern way of life.

She recollected the joy and anticipation reflected in her grandparents' eyes as she arrived along with her brother and parents, and the same eyes sad and teary with the pangs of separation as she and her family left for Mumbai.

To breathe the air of this charming village was exhilarating. The deep-water well in the sprawling lawn from where they still collected buckets of water, the garden with its banana and jackfruit trees—the whitewashed home always welcoming so many.

106

Her father would hold her hand and take her to every nook and cranny of the place. His lips turned to one side with a soft smile, his love for her and pride in her unhidden from her and the world.

At sunset, her sibling and cousins, along with her parents, uncles, and aunts who spruced up the atmosphere, would gather in the verandah and chant the sacred mantras together. Her grandmother would light the brass oil lamp, and they would pray and sing devotional songs. As the music pitch went from high to low, and then, low-to-high, Seema would experience a sense of divinity—the vibrations of the ages blending with the present.

The spectacular view from her grandmother's cottage overlooking the wavy, lacy paddy fields—the red fireball sun rising over the hills, the myna, the parakeet, the cuckoo, and the crows flying through the coconut palm fringes—the cool gentle breeze creating ripples in the ponds where the ducks and swans floated with not a care in the world, mesmerized her. The afternoon siesta, the simplest of life's pleasures, was a boon cherished by her uncles and aunts. Absorbing the beautiful sights of this untainted village was one of the childhood pleasures etched in Seema's memory. The ladies of the village, after a bath in the local pond or rivers, laid flower designs on their verandahs while men read the newspapers in the early morning hours—these were sensations that touched Seema. The drive through the villages, the enchanting temples, the cows grazing unfazed and unhurried, the chickens pecking at their food, the village kids running barefoot eating delicious mangoes plucked ripe from the deciduous trees and then dipping themselves into the village pond were scenes which never tired her. In this quaint village, when the monsoon season was in full swing, the rain-soaked soil with its fragrance cardinally touched her

107

soul; the fresh air, the sprouting saplings, the velvet green of the hills interspersed with streams, rivers gurgling eager to meet their beloved sea—the rising cliffs kissing the waves of water lapping around them were moments she cherished.

If these are not preserved for posterity, she thought, we will be left with a high-tech digital India, where no child will know the pleasures of nature, where mankind will crave for it with no respite in sight. That evening, while her husband was at work on his laptop, Seema penned an ode.

Ode to a village in India

A daughter born here

She is one of the most enchanting places in the whole wide world. Somewhere nestled in the heartland of the Western Ghats is a small village town. I was born in this dainty village. No place on earth beckons me a second time. But this village, untouched, rustic, never fails to enthrall me year after year with its luscious rice fields bordered by the mountains amongst which roaring waterfalls joined in merriment to form gurgling streams and rivers. This is where, as a child, I climbed the mango trees with friends and sang romantic songs as a young teen.

This is where we were taken by our mothers and aunts at dawn for a dip in the river and splash in the temple ponds. The banyan tree hiding the ancient temple still shades its deities. The numerous oil lamps in the temple, illuminating and fascinating in their piety.

As a kid, it was the grandparents who beckoned us to visit this quaint village. The long taxi drives speeding through the winding village roads from the railway station in the wee hours of the morning would leave me breathless as the rice fields with different shades of green fringed with coconut palms reveled and swayed carelessly. Today, again, my aging grandparents and my retired uncles and aunts beckon me.

I wake up early, eager to watch the sunrise from my grandmother's home, and am filled with awe as the red ball engulfs the fields and mountains and as the birds fly high through the trees and clouds chirping, welcoming a new day.

This little place on earth, unknown to most, remains the link between my childhood and my present—the traditional whitewashed homes, now adapting to more modern colors. The farm-fresh coconut curries mingled with fresh air somehow taste better here than anywhere else. Every year, I am amused to see the stones at the steps leading to the pond right where I saw it the previous year. Some things never change, even as we age, and that is my village—like the age-old banyan tree, my roots are deep-rooted in her soil. These invaluable trips have enriched me beyond what she will know. They have shaped me in a way unbeknownst to her.

Both my grandmother and grandfather belong to her in heart and soul.

I hope this village will retain her pristine beauty and values of friendship, support, and care for posterity and generations to come.

The villagers felt a sense of belonging to this village and the community.

A sense of belonging to a community was missing in the country she had been transplanted to.

The Suspicious Spouse

Seema was torn between her birth home and the adopted home. The birth home with all its miseries usually won over the adopted home with all its opulence. Such was the fate of many of the early immigrants.

After the long journey and the tricks her mind played, Seema went upstairs to her room. Sleep was the only respite from these thoughts. As she lay down, she sensed she was not alone. Her husband closed the bedroom door behind him. She shriveled into a fetal position and covered herself with a blanket.

"Remove your clothes."

She did not. She had not seen herself naked. She could not bear anyone else's prying eyes on her body. She hesitated. He could not understand. He was eager. Nobody disobeyed him. He got closer to her. He couldn't wait—he had waited long. He lifted her clothes, changed her position, and entered her. When it was over, he turned around and slept. She cringed. She could not touch herself. She had lost her virginity, which she had been told to guard with every fiber of her being, to her husband, a stranger. He would remain a stranger for the next two decades of her life. She did not sleep that night; tears rolled down her cheeks.

For the next twenty years, the same act was repeated, but twenty years later, the tears had dried up. She had accepted her fate along with the tirade of verbal abuse. Her days were spent cooking, cleaning, and raising the kids. Her nights were his to be ravaged as he pleased.

If any man complimented her, she would have to bear her husband's wrath. Accusatory words were thrown at her. "Whore," he would scream, seething with anger, and close the door. She would be left locked in the room. Famished, she worried about her kids, hoping they had eaten and praying they had gone to sleep. The next day when he opened the door reluctantly, still wanting to punish her, she went about casually—dutifully and responsibly doing her chores, not once asking for an explanation.

Sylvia had met Seema at a social gathering. There was sadness concealed in Seema's eyes, and Sylvia found herself drawn to this sad, forlorn woman.

Seema had been on the brink of taking her own life. She was nervous, scared, barely talking to anyone.

Her husband of many years was looking critically at her from across the room.

Sylvia approached her, taking in Seema's beauty, her thinning hair. They were about the same height. Her eyes were close-set, her lips thin, a long nose, but it was her peaches and cream complexion which made her stand out.

Men adored her, and women always gave her a second look. Nobody had fathomed the sorrow in her heart.

Somehow sadness was hardly ever associated with beauty.

"Hi, I am Sylvia."

"Seema."

"Is that your husband? He has been keeping a watch over you."

"Yes," she replied, averting her eyes from her husband and Sylvia.

"How long have you been married?"

"Twenty years." And then the story unfolded.

The Possessive Husband

Seema was his prized trophy. He had plucked a flower and transplanted her into his possession. She was young, naive of the worldly ways—this beautiful woman who was his wife now. 'How had he gotten so lucky?' Seema's husband wondered. His friends would be jealous, and he liked the thought.

Applauding himself, her husband smiled. At dinner, he would eat heartily, not noticing that she was just nibbling at the food on her plate.

Seema exuded a certain sensuality. Men desired her for her gentle demeanor; women found her winsome. They trusted her as their confidante.

During the early days of their marriage, exhausted after the daily chores, she would wait for her husband to come home so that they could go to the parks or stores or visit various places. She did not drive, and he did not encourage her to get a driving license. Her eagerness to explore the city ebbed as he made work an excuse not to take her anywhere. Soon her social contacts dwindled, parties and vacations became a rarity. He wanted her for himself.

He was egotistical and possessive.

She was lonely and depressed.

He abhorred her beauty, for it could tempt other men.

Her beauty had never given her joy.

He hated her for the love affair she never had.

She had no love lost for him.

He belittled her, intimidated her.

She bore the humiliation stoically and became the doormat he wanted her to be.

And yet, he found no solace.

She found no reason to live.

A few months after meeting Sylvia, who had averted her from committing suicide, Seema packed her bags and left her husband's house— the mansion which had taken her away from the poverty of her childhood and thrown her into a caged-princess existence. Without money or a job, she walked into an unknown future. She had few friends, and her parents were long dead. She had kept her misery to herself, veiled it from them so they could be spared the agony and worry and they had lived comforted by the thought that the apple of their eye was living the life of an opulent princess in the first world, a life they never had or could dream of. Their hearts swelled with pride when they thought of their luck and their dear daughter. This was their happy reality.

Her husband came home that fated night, his anger leveling off with age along with his appetite for sex. On his drive home, he had seen a couple kissing each other. Disgusted at the public display, he had looked away. The scene did manage to kindle a benevolent streak in him. He looked back at them and smiled to himself. He would take his wife to a restaurant that night. They had not been to a restaurant, just the two of them, since the kids were born. He rejoiced at the way he had molded her, pride surging through him. A new feeling of tenderness towards her warmed his heart. Her face had the lines of an older woman—the pain of the years had aged her prematurely. No man would be attracted to her. She would finally be his and his alone. He entered his home, feeling light and flippant for the first time in years.

He found a note on the doorstep. "I am leaving you, and you surely understand why."

He did not understand, had never understood her. He had only thought of himself.

He had provided for her, educated their children, occasionally taken the family on trips, though far in between. He had never laid eyes on another woman, then why, why had she left him now?

A sudden revelation dawned on him. Of course, he had been right all along. She was having an affair throughout the time she had been with him. He wondered why he had doubted his suspicions. It was crystal clear to him. She had run away with her lover. What he had worried about had happened. The 'bitch' he had meant to say the word under his breath, but it was so rambunctious that he was startled at the resonance.

He had prided himself with smugness over the power he had over her, his family, his workers; after all, he had built a successful business, provided jobs, educated his siblings after their father's early demise. He had harnessed the horses to victory, yet this ungrateful woman had left him.

He felt emasculated.

His siblings would mock him.

He felt defeated.

His workers would scorn him.

He would be the laughingstock of the society he had walled his home against.

It never crossed his mind that the chronic abuse had devoured her soul, that she hated daylight for it brought him to her vicinity—that she hated the night and cringed at his touch.

It never occurred to him that depression had so overwhelmed her that her mind was bereft of even a tiny space to contemplate an affair, that men were akin to devils in her world for the very few men she had known had not been kind to her.

His pride wounded, his prey gone; shattered and crushed, he had lost control over the one thing he had felt the need to subjugate lest she flies away. He cursed her headstrong beauty; he remembered her taunts, which he had quickly smothered. She had never made him feel like a man. She had never wanted him, had not responded to him. She, with all her beauty, had made him feel inferior, feel less of a man. Destitution engulfed him.

His inner isolation grew as his spurious external world crumbled.

As he ruminated, he felt relieved she was gone. He would not have to agonize about all the men who would be attracted to her.

Seema looked at the mirror in the hallway. The gregarious girl with an exuberant penchant for life had disappeared—the girl who had been free, who had run barefoot in the slushy rice fields, climbed the mango trees, braved the red ants on the trees, biting her with a vengeance when their territory was invaded, plucked mangoes from the strong barks had disappeared. Her childhood had disappeared—the flower her husband had picked had withered away. Her hair had thinned, the skin of her cheeks sagged, her eyes sunken, she was bulging at the seams. She did not recognize the face staring back at her.

Twenty years had passed by.

Twenty wasted years.

She tried to keep afloat through the whirlwind of thoughts. She was determined to make the rest of the years, worth their while.

"Aunty, what is the address you want me to drive you to?" the Bangladeshi taxi driver asked.

'Aunty' seemed to be generic for an older woman among people from the Indian subcontinent. She was irritated, 'why was he calling her aunty when his balding head made him look middle-aged? He must be in his forties,' she thought as she summed him up and grudgingly handed him Sylvia's address.

What Women All Over The World Need

And It Surely Is Not Designer Bags.

Sylvia opened the front door to let Seema in and hugged her. Once she made sure Seema was comfortable, Sylvia went into the kitchen to get a bottle of wine.

Opening the bottle of wine, excitedly, Sylvia said. "Well, well, I have a plan for you. You are getting yourself an education which will give you an income, and once you are independent, we will find you a date."

Seema could not stop smiling. "You seem to have thought of everything, and it sounds and looks so easy."

"It is as easy or difficult as you think it is. Maybe we can reverse the order, find a rich man, then get an education followed by work."

"Well, well," Seema imitated, "I did marry a rich guy, remember. The first suggestion seems better."

"Well, never mind. I will let you sleep. I have invited a few friends over tomorrow, just women. I do this every so often. We listen, vent, drink, eat, and go home ready to take on the world. It is our ritual to get through life and perhaps make some sense of it."

They trickled in one by one at noon, each bringing their favorite dish. It was their time to unwind. Miriam joined the group with some succulent fruit salad. Sylvia enjoyed this ritual. Seema, too looked forward to these women who seemed so accomplished and self-assured. She hoped their self-confidence would rub off on her. At the least, she found it a distraction from the upheaval her life was going through.

They spoke about the latest movies and TV shows. Sylvia rarely watched either. It numbed her senses and seldom left her feeling good. Most of the time, she got out of the theater feeling the pang of wasted time unless it was one of those artistic gems.

"Listen, ladies. This is Seema. She has just left her husband. We need to help her with some career goals and some good men," she added, hoping to lighten the scene.

"Marriage is the last thing I am interested in." Seema clarified, even as self-doubt tugged at her. Her lack of education and career made the feeling of insecurity worsen by leaps and bounds. Her college-going children lived busy lives, giving her no assurance. She might need to get married to secure her financial needs. This time she would choose carefully—she made a mental note, but not yet.

"Maybe I will introduce her to my father," one of the somewhat younger and newer members who hated her father's current girlfriend chimed in.

"Why did your mother pack up and take off, leaving you and your father?" came a direct question.

"Oh, it is a long story. Believe me. You don't want a stepmother. My father's girlfriend is so jealous that she hates to see me sitting or talking to my father. There is no love lost between us. I just want her out of my life, our lives."

"You know second marriages are difficult. About sixty-seven percent of second marriages end in divorce," opined another.

"Yes, there is the extra baggage you have to deal with in second marriages. His kids, her kids, his house, her house."

"What about the mother-in-law? My mother-in-law is so critical. She says, 'I have stolen her son for his money—that I have wrapped her son around me through sex, and that is why he listens to every whim and fancy of mine.'"

"You should put your foot down and not allow her to say such things."

"Lucky me. I don't have to. Her son detests her judgmental nature and all the turmoil she creates. She critiques him too for not taking care of her. The more desperate she is to hold onto him, the more she is losing him. She is so opinionated and trying to prove herself a victim in this saga that she is alienating me, her son, and her grandchildren. I will never be like her when I become a mother-in-law. I would accept the women my sons marry as my girls and not vie for my son's attention. The one quality I admire about my mother-in-law is her fierce independence. She doesn't depend on anybody and lives life at her terms."

"The best embellishment a person can wear is being nonjudgmental," Sylvia added.

"That is why you have a calming effect on people. You are so disarming," agreed another.

"Attention comes when you don't drag it towards you. You let go, you let them fly, and they come back because you have given them that space," came another opinion.

"I will not be that villain vying for my son's or daughter's affection. A son cannot be happy if he is torn between his wife and mother. That goes for the daughters too. Only when the couple is happy will I be happy. I would leave some of my opinions and ideas at home. Let them live their life as they want to. Let them learn from their mistakes," another friend chipped in her two cents.

"I hate my mother-in-law, and I believe the feeling is reciprocated," the mother-in-law hater added.

Another friend vocalized, "My mother-in-law is the nicest person I know. I respect her for her openness, her philosophy. She, more than my mother, has pulled me through the worst time in my life. She always encourages us and gives us advice on bettering our relationships, our careers. She says accepting and embracing others with all their flaws and goodness is the key to amity in relationships.

"All right, all right. I have a birthday cake," surprised another.

It was the mother-in-law hater's birthday.

"Thank you for the cake. But the wrinkles on my face seem to be marching with vigor and causing destruction in their wake."

"Oh, never mind them." The intellectual one brushed her off. "Here is a poem I wrote and published on aging, which I would like to read to you." She fished the poem from her phone and started reading.

121

"All right," Sylvia encouraged. "Let us have a poetry session before the cake cutting."

They sat in a circle, eager to hear.

Aging

As another year passes by, I was thinking about aging, and here are a few of my thoughts!

I thought age was a number until my kids called me 'antique.'
I smiled; after all, the antiques were priceless!

I thought age was a number until I shockingly saw the first wrinkle on my face.
I smiled; after all, it added character, and decided to embrace it!

I thought age was a number until I realized I had no more mountains to climb, no more ambitions to conquer.
I am. I exist.
I smiled and decided to float through life!

Everybody applauded her.

Another poem was brought out and read:

Aging

As I age, I surely must thank all of you for aging with me!

Age is just a numbers game, so play it.

Age is like vintage wine; it gets more valuable with time, so drink it.

Age is lines on your face; every line has a story to tell, so enjoy it.

Age is a phenomenon that spares no one, so accept it.

Age is sweet, spicy, tangy, so relish it.

"So true, but so hard to accept," said the unhappy one.

"What is happiness?" The question went around.

Sylvia brought out her write-up on 'Happiness,' which she had posted on Facebook. It had been well received.' "We all search for Happiness. I have combined some of my ideas on happiness with age-old wisdom."

"Here it is." She read it aloud.

Happiness

Happiness is being in harmony with oneself, others, and nature.

Happiness is having good relationships with people you interact with closely.

Happiness is a clean and clear conscience.

Happiness is contentment.

Happiness is a feeling of gratitude.

Happiness is being productive.

Happiness is good health.

Happiness is living within your means.

Happiness is living in the present moment.

Happiness is removing fear and worry from your mind.

Happiness is acceptance.

Above all, happiness is feeling good.

Her friends cheered. Encouraged, Sylvia brought out her diary in which she had written some nitty-gritty about life. She passed around the write-up, which she had written a few years ago. Some of the women read it, imbibing every word, some just did not have the patience, and some kept the article aside for some other time. Miriam, Sylvia's best friend, remained silent. The article read like this:

What Life Has Taught Me

I was engrossed in some soul searching at this fork of my life, contemplating how I had lived my life and the values which had shaped me.

I learned that it is imperative to accept another as he or she is.

Just as there are billions of unique faces, every personality is different.

Of course, thanks to the numerous permutations and combinations of the genetic pool, there is no face or personality which is not unique. I sometimes wonder at the billions of faces created by God.

A smile and the confidence you ooze are your best beauty accessory.

Do not judge another for when you do— you are saying to the other person that you are better than the other person. When you criticize another, you are just establishing your right to be right.

Friends become foes, and lovers come to hate each other, countries go to war, for we are unable to accept each other's differences.

Understand too that we cannot change anyone, not through love, critique, or punishment. Change has to come from within.

Money is important, contrary to what I was taught. But chasing money can be your worst enemy. Accumulate it ethically and let money chase you.

When we lived in a two-bedroom apartment, and since moving into a much bigger home, my mindset, my happiness quotient remained the same. The only difference is that now we have an alarm system and I know if we move to an even bigger home, the only difference would be that we would need a walkie-talkie to communicate with each other so I shall stay put! Yes, it is good to have space, but the happiness quotient does not increase.

Live within your means because, at the end of the party, you are the one left with the leftovers and the bills!

I have traveled extensively from the Canadian wilderness to down under New Zealand, not because I had the money, but I had the eagerness to do so.

Travel can be a beautiful, rejuvenating experience but can lead to weariness too.

If you want to sleep well, don't dance into the wee hours of the night, the adrenaline will keep you up.

Do not eat or drink wine before sleeping, for the sounds in your stomach will keep you up.

Keep your conscience clean. A pure heart, along with a hard day's work, will let you sleep through all the sounds of the world.

You do not have to please anyone. Just be yourself, for you are the only person you need to please. And others will like, love, and respect you for who you are. If they do not, it is their problem.

When people bully you or are mean to you, understand that they are hurting, stand tall, and do not waste a minute of your time on them. Even if it pinches, pinch yourself and know that it is a backhanded compliment.

You guys know the rest, eat healthy, exercise, and the like. All the above have come easily to me but for this last one.

I do not find the time to exercise, and I eat junk and feel guilty.

Oh, Sylvia, stop feeling guilty about food. I am sure there are other things you can waste your time feeling guilty about!

And oh, what about Facebook, Instagram, and the like. Though a great place to network, highlight your talents, market your product, brag about your kids, exhibit your vacations, and in an instant, reach thousands of voyeurs, studies show that social media and its like can lead to disconnect, discontent and even depression.

After all, social media is meant to showcase our smiles, our joys, our best.

Do we then seek help, reach out to a friend when we are having a sad day, a difficult month, or even a dreadful year when everybody appears so invincible on social media, so happy with life? Yes, this virtual reality is going to be the norm, and I am thrilled it exists. But sip it slowly.

Your identity cannot come through social media.

Enter the realm of social media cautiously. An adult mind may be able to differentiate between reality and virtuality, but it can be a different story for kids who are in their formative years, and I must say for many adults too.

So long.

The friends who read this article cheered on. "Maybe you should write a book," suggested one.

Jealousy With Its Fangs

One of the girls, Abigail, was not listening to the conversations. Her mind was preoccupied. She was thinking of her relationship with her father.

Abigail had been his solace when her mother had eloped with the bus driver who had dropped her every evening from work—deserting Abigail and her father. Abigail decided that she would never leave him. Her father waited for her through the wee hours of the morning as she returned from work. She rushed home to hug him. They went out for lunches and dinners together. A loner, his daughter, was the only world he had. Abigail never demanded anything from her father.

Time has a way of changing perspectives.

They were content with each other. Abigail felt secure for the first time in her life. She did not care anymore for frivolous clothes, shoes, or bags. The clutter was all around her. Her mother, who had bought these articles at her daughter's behest, had left her, and now Abigail did not care to wear any of them. She hated them. They were a reminder of their fights over what to buy, what suited her, how much they could afford. Once when her classmate had flashed the designer party wear and taunted her for her plain dress, she had screamed at her mother, accusing, "You don't love me. You want me to be humiliated."

"Is that what you think?" Her mother's sad face had turned pale. Those were her last words. There had been no time to mend.

She decided that with her father, everything would be different. She would never leave him, never demand anything of him, and she would be the person he leaned on. She dated a few men, but they were never as good as her father.

One day she came home and informed her father. "I have decided to quit my job. I want to be with you, look after you, spend time with you."

He was aghast. "I am fine. You should not do this. You need to focus on your career, your life." He slowly added, "I have found someone who will take care of me. She is a lovely woman."

There was silence as Abigail soaked in the news. Her life came crashing down. She was being abandoned again.

She hated this woman already. Jealousy, with its venomous fangs, spread its tentacles—searing pain ripped through her.

She could not focus. Everything became a blur. Her world collapsed.

"Am I not good enough? Don't I take care of you?"

"You are my daughter. I want you to have a life of your own. I want you to take on the world, marry, have kids, and give me grandkids. I don't want you to waste your life looking after me."

"How can you do this to me? You are selfish. I don't know how you can be happy abandoning me. She is after your money."

Abigail worried about her inheritance.

"I will make sure to leave enough for you," he assured her.

"That may not be a lot after she spends it all," Abigail retorted.

"You haven't met her," he reminded her.

"I cannot share you with her."

The years rolled by. Abigail stopped working and dating. Her mission in life was to oust her stepmother and regain her status as the queen of the house, the princess her father doted on. She fought with her stepmother—her stepmother fought back.

Abigail was crying over spilled milk, vying for attention, her loneliness projected as tantrums. Abigail and her stepmother stung each other with venom—their need to be right overshadowing any compromise. They each felt a victim where the other was manipulating a siege—they scrimmaged to wall off their loved one from the other.

Her father re-entered the realm of isolation. Depression from which he had tried to disencumber himself pulled him back into its vortex.

The stepmother caved in. She was quiet for a while, barely retaliating back. Her husband became morose, and his mood swings did not help her either. She left him. She left the stepdaughter. He had not supported her enough, she accused.

Abigail was overjoyed. She had won the war. Her father belonged to her now—his money would be hers to enjoy. She did not have to share him with anyone. She would not share him with anyone.

She smiled at her reflection in the mirror, the smile of a victor—the smile vanished as soon as it came upon her face. The years of strife had taken a toll. There were gray hairs peeping through the sides of her face, her face haggard—she clutched at the sinking feeling in the pit of her stomach. All these years, her attention was focused on getting rid of the woman who had married her father. With that accomplished, she was at leisure to think about herself. Her appearance appalled her. She screeched, desperate to evade the devastation that grappled her. How had this happened? Who would marry her were her thoughts as she threw a paperweight to break the reflection into pieces?

That night Sylvia wrote:

Animosity and hate towards another never leave the bow. The arrow destroys the carrier and embers the surroundings.

Sylvia decided to watch a late-night comedy to divert her mind.

'Thank God for these comedians life was worth laughing at.'

She found in them and their satire one of the highest forms of intelligence. She watched 'The Colbert Report' that night.

People:

Complex, Complex, Complex!

People Should Come With The Label, 'Handle With Care. Very Fragile.'

The day after the gathering, Sylvia went to work, feeling groggy. Little did she realize that another challenge was awaiting her.

The director to whom she had been reporting for the last five years had resigned. He had mentored Sylvia, and over the years, they shared a deep trust in each other. It had not been easy for Sylvia to see him leave the institution. She threw a huge farewell party for him. He had groomed Sylvia to take charge of his role and had confidently seconded her name to the position. Sylvia was appointed as the interim director.

One of Sylvia's male colleagues was upset when she was selected for the interim director position. "They are just using you. I think you should withdraw from the position."

Another male colleague confronted her, "I don't think you're fit for the position."

The elation Sylvia had felt at being selected as the interim director deflated like a balloon pricked and crumpled.

"Those men are insecure." Her husband of a few months remarked. It had made her feel better. Mark, her husband, was an unassuming man, not ambitious nevertheless worked hard at whatever he did. He was of medium height, thick blond hair, and blue eyes, which spoke volumes of philosophy though he had read none. His lips were thick below his pug nose. One day she would look into his ancestry, she told herself—he was all-American, but she was sure there were native Indians and people of color in his lineage. Perhaps the blue eyes had dominated the generations.

Sylvia quickly realized that her dream of becoming the director would be thwarted by these insecure men who had started their careers at the university almost at the same time as she had. 'At least she had been selected over them. That was perhaps some consolation.'

The Bully

A few days later, the dean introduced her to the permanent director of the department. "This is Dr. Ann Smith. She is joining us as the new director. She has many years of experience." The dean somehow felt the need to give an excuse as to why he had chosen Dr. Smith over Sylvia.

Sylvia stood up and greeted her with the effusive joy of meeting a stranger.

The dean was pleased with her attitude; he went on to add, "Sylvia will be able to teach you the ropes. She is very efficient."

Sylvia felt Dr. Smith's eyes piercing her. The friendliness in them was replaced by apprehension. The apprehension that her place of power would be supplanted by 'the efficient lady.' She was gauging Sylvia. Sylvia looked at Dr. Smith, who was about five feet two inches tall, obese, with short straight, sparse hair tied in a ponytail, a large nose, her ears protruded out of her face on either side like flaps. She wore thick myopic glasses. Her hips were the largest part of her body, broad and jutting out of the torso. She wore a pale pink shirt tucked into her bright pink slacks. Her shoes were velcroed onto her small feet.

Sylvia vacated the interim director's desk and room, took her belongings, and walked to her old desk.

"This desk is taken," her male colleague putting his hand across the desk, made it clear, adding, "I told you they were using you."

Sylvia did not utter a word. She let him take her old desk. "Is there any empty desk where I can keep my stuff?" She enquired loudly. A female colleague guided her to one. "Thank you," Sylvia said as she placed her bag on the desk. Suddenly her becoming the interim director had brought with it a lot of hostility, palpable to almost everyone and, most of all, to Sylvia herself.

Dr. Smith did not want any looming threats to her chair. 'Some heads will have to roll, she told herself, but she would have to be discreet.'

Dr. Smith had grown up bearing the brunt of jibes. She rarely looked at herself in the mirror—her reflection, too, seemed to mock her, tease her. In the eighth grade, she realized that her appearance was weird. She looked different from her classmates. Some of them sneered at her, and others intimidated her; some pulled her protruding ears. She cried, secretly hating herself. A black-dense cloud of darkness clung to her heart. Brutally chained by the shackles of her dark emotions, she failed to understand what it was to be happy, what it was to be at peace.

The Gods she cried to had finally relented. She had been given this position of power. The dean of the university had a daughter studying under the tutelage of Dr. Smith's father, and he had obliged. Dr. Smith's father, a wealthy philanthropist, had bestowed an endowment of $500,000 to the university. "I hope you understand that Ann deserves this position," were her father's words for the selection committee.

Dr. Smith entered her private office, breathing in the smell of fresh paint, touched the shiny mica on the large wooden desk feeling a surge of power lighten her heart fleetingly. She knew this was her chance to chasten her bullies, to avenge her unhappiness.

'Oh, how long had she waited for this power—to get her sweet vengeance. All those treacherous years were not in vain. It was her turn. She would have the last laugh. She would look for the vulnerable ones, she thought. She would weed out the odd ones and purify the department. She would ruin anybody who stood in her way.'

For the first time in years, she felt invincible. She went home exhilarated, happy, wondering why such beautiful feelings had never crossed her mind till then. She remembered the deriding remarks of the girls in her school—

they had teased her for being the person with strange facial features. The laughter of the boys echoed in her ears, crushing her.

She checked out the people she was responsible for. She would choose her victims carefully. She prided herself at the thought, 'wondering why she usually lacked conviction, was diffident about her abilities. Why did she loathe herself? This time she would prove to the world how valuable she was professionally and personally, and above all, she would prove to herself her worthiness.'

Somehow everything was falling into place, and she felt smugly satisfied. She thought of Sylvia being her first victim. 'No,' her self-talk began. People may get suspicious. After all, she and Sylvia had vied for the same position.

She would target the person Sylvia had been slighted by the day she had joined the university. He had appropriated Sylvia's chair and space. He was one of the contenders for Sylvia's position. Maybe he would want her chair next.

"I am letting go of Samir," she told the dean the next day. "Why?" the dean asked, somewhat surprised. Samir was not an exceptional worker but had always met expectations. The dean had believed in mentoring rather than terminating people. Terminating people was expensive and time-consuming, and he cared about his staff.

"It is not easy to terminate someone here. We would need a paper trail."

She had a ready answer, "We can lay him off. I checked our budget. We don't have enough for his salary. We are short of funds."

"Oh, you have analyzed the budget; that is impressive."

"Yes, I have."

"Since you have been so thorough, it is your call," he replied, not wanting to influence or interfere with her work.

"Thank you," she beamed, pleased that he was on her side and had been impressed by her.

A feather in her cap, she strutted down the corridor, wondering why she kept doubting her smartness.

After her first victory, armed with the power it gave her over the bullies of the past, and the peers of her present, Dr. Smith, began to focus her attention on Sylvia. She would go over Sylvia's work with a microscope in an effort to find some flaws.

Sylvia, uncomfortable with this intrusion, accelerated her efforts to achieve perfection. She did not want merely to be 'meets expectation.'

She wanted to be 'exceeds expectation,' but then institutions and corporations keep increasing their expectations, and Dr. Smith did just that.

The Corporate Existence

Dr. Smith went to Sylvia's immediate boss, Ryan. Surely, he would have something negative to say.

His elucidation disappointed her. "Sylvia works extremely hard. I have told her many a time if she continues like this, her health might suffer."

Ryan had joined the university burnt out by the corporate world, a world where he had worked endless hours and received a six-figure salary, promotions, cars, houses.

He had worked himself to the bone, prioritizing his job over his family.

Nothing was ever enough for the corporations. They want more and more. They are pressed to satisfy their board members and shareholders.

If the company is profitable, they wanted more—if the company is in the red, they needed more from the staff to survive.

The human in between was getting crushed—the human mind was getting penalized. People were bringing work home or staying late at work. Such was the work culture being propagated. Standards were being raised all the time, and sometimes impossible and impractical standards were imposed. The effect was that nobody was ever good enough for the corporate world.

Grueling work hours, slave-driving employers, the dissatisfaction crept in gradually and surreptitiously overwhelming his mind and soul.

Ryan had internalized his frustrations. He brought work home, and along with it, pent-up anger. He felt entitled when he got home.

The children would quietly retire to their rooms to avoid his wrath. His wife would greet him with a half-smile and then try her best to avoid his path. She would strive to make him happy, cooking the dishes he liked. Sometimes the food on the plate along with the plate would come flying at her. "There is too much salt. I work so hard for all of you. Can't a man expect a decent meal?" His home was the only place where he felt in charge. The more he felt in control, the more his need to control increased. The children would cling to their mother, unable to bear their mother's tears.

He had become this devil at home in stark contrast to the very obedient vice president at work.

He even started enjoying this devilish side of his. The more scared his wife and children were, the more he secretly relished and indulged in this behavior till one day, his teenage son threw the plate back at him. The boy was taller than him. The plate hit his head. There was blood all over. His family took him to the hospital. Everybody was quiet. No charges were made. His wife forbade it. The only people at his bedside were his wife and kids. What was in the family remained in the family.

140

The dynamics changed. He left the corporate job, went in search of peace. He found it in bits and pieces. His quest remained unfulfilled.

He mentioned his 'spiritual seeking' failures to Sylvia. "One day, maybe I should go to India, maybe the Himalayas, and find a Guru."

She replied coolly. "Peace is within you. Just as you had unleashed your anger, unleash the peace within. I was in India a few years ago, and I have seen joy and laughter in the slums of Mumbai and misery in the mansions of Manhattan. Somewhere in the rat race, we scuttled like the mice, wanting more and more of the pie, tripping each other, creating chaos and friction. In our need to complete ourselves, we usurped energy from each other. We tried to control by creating fear. This is what others do to us, and we tend to retaliate in the same way, with similar behavior. Hurt begets hurt. This is true of all relationships."

Ryan wanted to continue the conversation. Sylvia sensed his disgruntlement as she looked at the clock.

"I am getting late for the meeting."

"We should continue our conversation. I like talking to you." Ryan let her know.

How To Create Rifts And Misunderstandings?

As Sylvia entered Dr. Smith's office, she found Dr. Smith restlessly pacing the room.

"Call me Ann," she said, pointing her finger towards the chair, bidding Sylvia to sit.

Dr. Smith knew she had to lay a bait for Sylvia. She kept hearing good things about Sylvia from everyone; a motivated worker, an eager learner, always there for me, vast knowledge. Dr. Smith searched for that one flaw in Sylvia, which she could exaggerate and shatter her with.

"How is Janet?" she asked Sylvia. "Janet, the Asian girl," alluded Dr. Smith.

Janet and Sylvia had been working together for over a year. Janet had still not grasped and seemed disinclined to learn the job. Sylvia had to work harder and cover-up for Janet's lack of knowledge about the subject. Sylvia had wanted to broach this with someone, and this seemed an opportune moment. "Janet's aloof and does things at a slow pace. She doesn't commit herself to complete the tasks. I have to pick up the slack."

Little did Sylvia realize that the bully had found her bait. Joyous, Dr. Smith immediately went to Janet and informed her about these accusations Sylvia had made in implied confidence.

Janet snapped back, belligerent. "Sylvia plagiarizes all my research work and notes." She went on a combative spree, ranting and lying about Sylvia's work ethic.

"Will you let the dean know this?" Dr. Smith asked in a calm tone.

"Of course," came the acrimonious reply.

The bully had pitted the two against each other. She had sparked the fire of antipathy.

Janet had always been an angry child, dismayed by her 'fresh off the boat' parents who spoke English mixed with a heavy accent, who sold their food at makeshift tents for a living. Torn between her parents being an embarrassment as she tried to fit into western society, she despised the likes of Sylvia, who seemed to have it all.

"Come, come," Dr. Smith held Janet's hand and dragged her at a fast speed, almost tripping her to the dean's office.

Dr. Smith was thrilled. She had manipulated, pitched two people against each other, and concocted an accomplice for herself. She applauded herself for outwitting Sylvia. 'Surely, the dean would recognize her strength and Sylvia's weakness.' The bully was in a position of power, and Sylvia would be the next pawn. The spider spun the web.

Janet, who had not stopped being angry at the world for causing her shame blurted out all the fabrications, she could think of, vilifying Sylvia to the dean.

Ryan, Sylvia's immediate boss, was called in. He was puzzled. The dots seemed disconnected. Disturbed by these allegations, he felt a gnawing sense of fabrication; something was amiss. The dean paced around, disconcerted. It was his responsibility to investigate, his obligation to give the benefit of the doubt to the director he had hired.

The Husband

Sylvia was mortified by the events unfolding at work. For the next three months, she went to work every day, even on weekends, rain, or snow. Work had become her life, her breath, a place where she could focus and forget herself, despite the rest of the faculty animatedly discussing her predicament. Work was the solace, an excuse to retain her sanity. It was when she got into her car and drove home that trepidation would overwhelm her. She was working hard to get tenured, which was getting to be a difficult task akin to finding a needle in the haystack—almost impossible.

It perplexed her that the dean had continued to test her despite his reservations.

She would come home to Mark, who would have some hot tea ready for her. Massaging her stiff shoulders and tight neck, he said, "Babes, you are going to be fine. Just don't criticize the bully. Don't say anything to anyone"

Dr. Smith's name had become synonymous with the bully. "Walls have ears, and they will talk, even the most trustworthy of them—it will reach her, instigate her to gear up more ammunition against you. Critiquing would only create more enemies and abate the support you can garner."

Sylvia was in awe of this man's wisdom. He had not read a book in his life—his passion lay in politics and current affairs. To her, his intrinsic worth far outweighed the extrinsic definition of success. He was not part of the six-figure salary club to which she belonged. But he had never let that diminish him or his self-esteem.

Self-esteem hardly seems to be the byproduct of money, education, position, power, or looks. Self-esteem was a manifestation of self-worth—the ability to understand ones worth, a feeling of security with what and where one is. Self-confidence was accepting one's imperfections along with the strengths and understanding that they went hand in hand.

Mark had a quirky, witty side to him that made her laugh, lightening her heart, her soul, and their home. Laughter was the kaleidoscope coloring their lives during these trying times. Somehow the torment at work was alleviated by his presence at home. The moonlight bathed their room.

Watching this eternal symbol of love, she slowly sipped the tea, smiling at him, "You're my pillar, my strength, my support."

Mark had become the anchor she leaned on for every small disturbance her mind went through—his perspective became her mantra, reassuring her.

He stood stoically by her.

She had become an extension of him.

They were entwined together.

"Well, well, babes, do you need anything from me? I cannot buy you diamonds." She threw a pillow at him, and he dodged, laughing. She moved towards him, yearning to touch him, gravitating towards him like a flowing river becoming one with the ocean.

"Cupid from heaven is pleasuring you."

She smiled in agreement; he was a giver, and her wild response flamed his amatory inclinations.

In her diary, she wrote:

Love has a way of lifting you from despair, from agony. The train of thought when one is in love encompasses the mind with ruminations of the lover that every other contemplation falls by the wayside. His love and her feelings for him had not just sustained her but had made her come alive with a force that overcame all negativity, the lies, the poison that the director was throwing at her. All the slings and arrows had to penetrate the halo surrounding her, and they failed.

The next day armed with love, she went to work. She was at work in all her splendor, dressed casually but looking lovely — hair all over her face, adding to her appeal.

She glowed, somehow love glowed.

The dean called her into his office. She could take anything today, even the pink slip. As she walked into his office, she imagined herself 'tearing the pink slip into the air and walking out of the campus. The students and the faculty, standing next to her with tears in their eyes, bidding her farewell.'

She entered the dean's room. He was amazed to see her look so radiant.

He wanted to tell her, 'You look so pretty.' Instead, he stuck to the lines he had rehearsed. "I know what is going on," implying his knowledge of the wicked ways of the bully.

A barrage of words came out of Sylvia's mouth. "Well, I'm glad you know, and if I have worked well with you, then protect me."

Self-preservation was man's first instinct, and she was preoccupied with safeguarding hers.

As Sylvia walked out of the dean's room, an administrator came up to her and remarked, "You have a fan club. Stand tall and strong."

Another colleague went up to her and hugged her. "You are such a gem of a person. These people will drive you crazy. I believe in you," he reassured her.

"These things happen in America," a senior professor from the English department mocked at the system.

One by one, the staff and her colleagues began to comprehend the situation. Sylvia was competent, and her peers liked working with her. They slowly became cognizant of the bully's nefarious mind and the discrepancies in the allegations. As the faculty were unable to fathom or justify the accusations flung at Sylvia, the bully desperately schemed to vindicate herself.

She vehemently searched for another accomplice and found it in her friend and confidante. She spotted her friend walking pompously down the hallway, wearing colorful clothes. Momentarily, the bully hesitated, not sure of sharing her losing battle with Sylvia, and then the words poured out. The confidante acquiesced.

Dr. Smith was in a position of power. Supporting Dr. Smith, her confidante felt—would mean getting a faster promotion and help her remain in good standing. Sylvia was just an assistant professor with no administrative clout. Dr. Smith's confidante went to the faculty and lied about Sylvia.

This time, however, the faculty had seen through Dr. Smith and the falsities of her confidante.

Dr. Smith felt her world slither away. Desolation set in. She needed to exonerate herself from the pain. Her head screamed, 'she would gather more people, spread stories, and ruin Sylvia's career.' She was not ready to concede.

She called Sylvia into her office. "The ball is back in your court. Is this how you do things?"

Sylvia was not sure what Dr. Smith had meant.

Wiser now, Sylvia remained quiet. Her husband's words echoed. "Never say anything to the bully. Your words will be misconstrued, spiced up, and presented in an ill fashion. She will twist your words and use them against you."

Some people who are hurting inside find ruthless retribution through malevolence and harm to others. Of course, there are others who have been hurt but evolve, find salvation in helping people who are going through pain.

For Sylvia, this had not been a game. It had been her livelihood, her survival ticket. She had regained her career, which had come to fruition after years of effort, without uttering a malicious word against the director. She had persevered.

"You have won," the bully said. When it was over, Sylvia left Dr. Smith's office without a word.

Sylvia did not feel like a winner. She had gotten her life back, which had been placed on hold for the last two years.

In these trying times, Sylvia heeded her husband's words. He had been the prop she leaned on, the voice of wisdom she soaked in. She loved him more than ever.

Sylvia never looked back, felt no anger for the way she had been treated. Love had not allowed anger to sprout despite the injustice the bully had thrown at her.

As for the bully, she could fool the rest of humanity only for so long. Her peers did not give her any credence. They had lost their trust in her, the facade had fallen, and Dr. Smith became the butt of jokes and object of ridicule by her peers once again. She despised them, painfully aware of their animosity towards her. They were part of a world she could never hope to reach or touch. She detested Sylvia for catapulting her into this crevasse, the flame of anger burning her core.

Meanness never brought any respite with it.

It created an uphill battle with oneself.

Vacation

Sylvia needed to get away from the pandemonium her work life had just gone through.

"Let's go to the mountains, away from all this chaos," she said as she plunked herself onto the sofa, exhausted not from physical disease but the mental exhaustion created by her tumultuous thoughts. A new place was thrilling. The roads, the people, the smells, the sights were stimulating in their novelty, which diminished with familiarity. Someone had said familiarity breeds contempt. Sylvia had found this to be most true when exploring places, rarely visiting the same place twice.

Cruising the vast seas, watching history unravel its architectural splendor, the exotic beauty of the crystals, creatures, geysers, and the rock formations boastful of their glory, glorious in their magnificence, was akin to being a curious witness to the eons of the past.

They went to the Blue Mountains in Pennsylvania. It was a memorable trip.

Gazing at the Blue Mountains, Sylvia wrote:

The Blue Mountains

The Blue Mountains stood tall in all their glory. The air was crisp and cold, touching my face. The sky was changing from golden yellow to orange and then magenta. I stood there watching this spectacle like a stubborn child despite the cold breeze hitting my face.

The red robin was flapping her wings. Her mate was ardently pursuing her. The robin ducked into the bushes, almost teasing the mate.

The scene kindled some memories of yesteryears of someone saying, 'Please do not leave yet, my heart is not filled yet.'

I remembered my first blush, pretending to be unaffected yet relishing the sincerity with which those words were spoken. The memory, a faint blur now, somehow resurfaced and brought a smile to my face.

I steadfastly watched the mesmerizing play of the setting sun against the Blue Mountains. The lake at the edge of the valley was calm and tranquil. The cold wind was blowing my hair. I could not move. I did not want to move. This display of God's earth, the wild wind, the majestic mountains, the melody of the forest, the serenity of the lake were beckoning me.

The deer were grazing in the meadows. One of them looked at me with caution. 'I am just as scared of you as you are of me,' I thought. The deer walked away. 'I am as harmless as you are,' I wanted to say.

Suddenly a few more deer joined their lone companion, and together they moved away gracefully. They were going home. I watched this spectacle.

The sun had hidden behind the mountains. Dusk was falling over the ranges. I could see only the silhouette of the mountain ranges now.

The slit moon was peeping from above—the multitude of stars twinkled in the night sky, the crickets were croaking, celebrating life.

The lights flickered in the valley.

I walked into the room hesitantly. The warmth of the fireplace wrapped me as I walked in.

The husband looked at my flushed face, smiling. I was not sure if he understood. It did not matter. I smiled back at this simple man who had become the pillar I leaned on and who invariably made me laugh with his quirky jokes. I was home too.

Earth, Water, Fire was all there in you, Blue Mountains.

I will never have enough of you. 'My heart is not filled yet.'

The Best Friend

The day they returned from their vacation, Sylvia found a message on the answering machine from her friend Miriam. Miriam was this cheerful, gregarious, fun-loving, bubbly schoolmate. She was tall, fair with long black hair, the beauty of their class. Beauty and vanity sometimes went hand in hand but not with Miriam. She rarely identified herself with beauty.

Miriam had spent her childhood in India. Later, her parents had moved to Dubai, which was a haven for many people from Asia. Dubai was an escape to an affluent lifestyle with its larger-than-life malls, magnificent structures surrounded by water, and palm trees in the middle of the desert—gold and silver hung from its shops. The whole city would light up during the festivities. People roamed its streets shopping and merrymaking late into the night. The oppressive heat with extreme humidity made it impossible to work in the afternoons. This was the time when people took long breaks and naps in the comfort of their air-conditioned homes only to restart work in the evenings.

When Miriam was in her teens, her parents, like most people from the Indian subcontinent, had to make a choice—'move back to India or go to America to educate their children.'

The wealthy usually were able to get a visa to America. Miriam's parents decided to move to America when she completed high school. It was not a smooth transition. Her father had worked as a medical doctor in Dubai for many years. In the US, his medical degree was not recognized— nor his years of experience validated. The money he had made in Dubai would run out if he did not work. The dollar was too strong against the currency he brought with him and the expenses a lot more. He became a phlebotomist, drawing blood in the lab, earning a near minimum wage.

Miriam was his hope, his passage to the dream of becoming a doctor in America, wearing the white coat, without which he felt utterly lost.

He shed tears of joy when he bought her her first white coat as she walked through the corridors of the medical school.

When she went into her class, he had cried with convulsing pain, the pain of having his career, his calling stymied and crushed by the system, yet grateful that his daughter would become a doctor and achieve his dream of wearing the 'white coat' in America. He vicariously lived his thwarted dream through his daughter.

His wife held his hand, "Your sacrifice has not gone to waste. She will carry your legacy forward. We came to the United States to give our children a better life, and she has already proven herself."

She wiped his tears. He smiled through his tear-filled eyes, unable to contain his pride.

Miriam, Sylvia, and Emma became thick friends during the sophomore year of college. They were naughty

155

pranksters, with Miriam leading the pack. Their teachers loved and hated them.

Sylvia remembered the words of one of the teachers. "Miriam was here for two years. She aced the class, won all the accolades, leaving others behind." The teacher had said this with pride and a heart full of joy.

Miriam had no desire to leave others behind. The fire which propelled her was a frenetic aspiration to be the best in class. She would lock herself in a room and pore over books.

Partying and hanging out were placed on a back burner, not enjoyed the few times they were tended to. She would want to rush home and be in the company of her scholarly books.

Nothing was ever achieved without a fire in the belly and focused attention on the goal.

Once Miriam joined the medical school, she had been too busy. With different careers, Sylvia and Miriam's paths had taken different turns till many years later, thanks to a WhatsApp group started by one of their classmates—they renewed their friendship.

A few months later, in the winter, Miriam and her parents planned to visit Miriam's grandparents in Lucknow, India.

They invited Sylvia to join them. For Sylvia, this was a dream come true. She was excited to join Miriam on the trip to Lucknow and Agra for a week.

Lucknow was a city of ancient architectural splendor. Sylvia was awe-struck by some of the palaces and courts she saw. Later in the night, as was the norm with her, she wrote about a historical structure in Lucknow, India.

It took my breath away!
If the Taj Mahal is a unique expression of love unmatched in this world for its overwhelming beauty, I feel the Bada Imambara is a unique monument with its acoustic, scientific, and architectural splendor.
The sound of a paper being torn or a match being lit is amplified multiple times to be heard 300 meters away. Sound travels through its walls as if through the telephone wires of today. The expression ' Walls have ears' perhaps originated here. Ingenious ways of getting to the enemy before they got to you!
I could not but stop and thank the Emperors and Kings of yesteryears for creating such a feast for the eyes.
Hope we continue to preserve and enjoy it.

The next day, Miriam and Sylvia went strolling in the parks of this ancient city, a city where poetry and literature were inherent in its culture.

In one of the parks, a saintly man dressed in a saffron robe was giving a discourse. About 200 people were listening to him. He was talking about the oneness of humanity. Sylvia was mesmerized. She was curious. She decided to stay back at the guru's ashram for a few days, which got extended for a few months, much to Mark's displeasure, who eventually joined her. She called the human resources department at her university and applied for a sabbatical year.

Sylvia immersed herself in the rituals and traditions of the ashram. This is where she was exposed to the age-old wisdom, which intermingled with modern-day existence.

She learned about the elements needed to lead a peaceful life and returned to the United States, cheered and empowered by what she had learned, ready to impart the message.

Sylvia and Mark landed at the JFK airport in New York on a cold, wintry, snowy day in January after a 20-hour journey from the tropics, flying over lands and seas—their minds in a daze by the change in scene, the still snow juxtaposed against the noise and warmth of the country they had left behind. Twenty hours ago, when they had boarded the plane, the sun was shining bright, and the air of the tropics was warm.

Miriam was at the airport waiting to receive Mark and Sylvia after their year-long sojourn. They were happy and relieved to be driven home at that late hour, after the long flight. Miriam's familiar face brought joy after a year of being away from New York.

Miriam was eager to hear their stories. She took them to a restaurant where they ate, laughed, and animatedly shared some of their experiences with Miriam until jet lag hit Sylvia hard. "I will give you insights into spiritual immersion, some other time," Sylvia teased, trying hard to keep her eyes open. Mark put his hand around Sylvia.

Miriam could not help but observe the love between Mark and Sylvia. As Miriam drove them home, she remarked, "Mark and you are so much in sync with each other."

Sylvia smiled.

Married Love

It can be as deep as the ocean, as still as a serene lake. Secure and calm, the graying hair or the aging, fine lines on the face matter no more. This time it is not an exclusive bubble. The euphoric intoxication gives way to cozy affection. Married Love is sedate but comforting compared to the first rush of a heady, giddy love when you fall in love with a stranger. It includes everything else, or it can be otherwise.

Mark was away that weekend. Sylvia missed him—every minute, they were not together. If he was late, she missed him; if he was tending to the garden and she was preparing lunch in the kitchen, she missed him. The little time they had after work, she would hover around him, chatting with him, listening to his wisdom, his views on politics, on history.

A documentary was shown on TV about how a man from the Middle East had come to America, was appalled by the open society, gone back home, and spread anti-American views on morality. The American presenter had claimed that fundamentalism had spread its tentacles influenced by this one man.

159

"Hmm..." her husband had ventured. He went on to quote history and talk about the centuries-old religious conflicts, the decades of Israel-Palestine conflict, and the deadly Syrian war.

His opinions paved the way for animated chats with her four lunch buddies at work. Brian was one of the lunch buddies. He had a clean-shaven head and worked in the Math department. He would join them in the cafeteria.

Somehow, in their eagerness to meet, they managed to get out at the same time for lunch, keen on discussing the current affairs and the economy. Sylvia would express her husband's viewpoints; the four of them would talk enthusiastically about the economy and world affairs. Her lunch buddies were eager for more. They admired her knowledge—she, in turn, adored her husband's insights.

One day she acknowledged to Mark: "You have interesting things to talk about. I enjoy your input and perspectives and worldly views!"

He smiled lovingly and added, "I have to go to Boston for a few days. I have to speak at a seminar. Would you like to join me? We can drive together."

"I have just come out of the grind, albeit unscathed, but I better work and prove myself."

He smiled again, hiding his disappointment this time. He had hoped to make a family road trip when his boss told him about the presentation the next day, "I think you have proved yourself. I will be away until next Tuesday." He kissed her forehead and went inside to pack.

'I love you. Thank you for being mine. Thank you for being there for me,' Sylvia thought without putting them into words, wondering why she had not voiced her thoughts.

160

We are so vociferous when we criticize our loved ones but mute when it comes to expressing love.

Did she fear it would sound overbearing or make him a bit arrogant?

She made a mental note to voice her admiration for him. Praiseworthy words were a form of encouragement, enhancing relationships. The age-old adage that it could lead to vanity was not true after all.

A Day At The Beach

It was a cloudy, warm Saturday. Sylvia had no plans for the day, and with Mark away, she was feeling somewhat lost figuring out what to do with her day off. Over two years of togetherness left her uncomfortable when she was alone. She had gotten used to having him around. As she reflected, she realized she had not been in contact with her friends. It had been a year since she had met them. Her train of thoughts included Neil. She wondered how he was doing and curbed a sudden urge to call him.

Men had a way of misunderstanding phone calls, misunderstanding friendships. She did not want him to misconstrue and believe that she was rekindling a romantic rendezvous.

The phone rang. She intuitively knew it was Neil. His voice was shaking. "I want to talk to you. How have you been? Can I come over? Is your husband home?"

"Neil, is everything ok?" She queried, concerned. He had let out an array of questions, and she did not know where to begin. Mark was not home, but she did not want any complexities. She did not want Neil to come over.

162

"Why don't we meet at the beach?" She felt safer there, almost justified.

"Great idea, see you at 4 pm." She heard the exuberance in his tone and smiled to herself.

She was at the beach an hour early, wearing a tank top and shorts, her eyes wide from a good night's sleep. She had put on a warm-hued lipstick—usually the only makeup she wore and slipped into her slippers. Feeling pleased with her petite figure, she drove to the beach.

She stood at the edge of the water, basking in the sun, watching the waves lapping onto the rocks and sand. She loved the way the waves eroded the sand under her feet as they ebbed back into the ocean. The seagulls seemed to be celebrating life, flying in flocks, flapping their wings, chirping, hunting for food, diving into the water, and coming out triumphantly with their prey.

Kids were playing, building castles in the sand, splashing against the waves, and then running towards their parents in need of reassurance as their parents sunbathed, relaxed while keeping an eye on the kids as they ran back into the ocean.

The vastness of the ocean was meditative—nothing seemed to matter other than the waves and herself. Every strife was forgotten at that moment. She gazed at the ship afar, the boats languorously sailing on the surface of the water.

Someone had interpreted the world as being round by watching the ships disappear from his line of vision and had been persecuted for that truthful discovery.

'The world was stranger then,' she thought.

"Hi stranger," a familiar voice interrupted her thoughts. She felt a bit nervous as she turned around, "Hi Neil."

"It is such a pleasure to see you. You have not changed, just as pretty," he lauded her.

"Thank you, Neil. How have you been?"

"I am well," he replied, unsure of his well-being.

They made small talk for a while, ignoring their curiosity about each other's life.

Finally, Sylvia ventured, "Have you found a girlfriend?"

"Not really," he said, his eyes sparkling with adoration for her.

She was not sure what 'not really' meant.

"You are an attractive man; rather, you can attract women."

It was his turn not to understand what she meant. "What do you mean?"

Three kinds of men

"There are three kinds of men," Sylvia went on enjoying herself.

"The first kind of men were those whose eyes rarely revealed anything. If they cared for a woman, it was hardly apparent to their love interest, to the woman of their dreams. Such men could be handsome, high achievers in their own way or otherwise but were neither articulate nor let their eyes do the talking. They found it hard to get the woman they liked. They were shy and feared rejection.

"The second kind of men looked at women lecherously. Their insecurity about themselves projected in their eyes—in their need to harass or overpower women. Women cringed from such men, hid themselves, hid their breasts, and whatever else they could from their prying eyes.

"Then there is the third kind of men who were just inept at hiding their admiration for the woman they adored. They had the gift of the gab and the gift of their expressive eyes. Their voice may not push out words of love, but it was enunciated and proclaimed in the modulation of their tone. Their eyes spoke far more words than their lips articulated. Women found their reflection in the eyes of such men to be stunning. Somehow, they could make a woman feel beautiful, desired, cherished, and adored—all without a word. They made the woman fall in love with herself."

He chuckled, "God, I miss you."

She ignored that. "So, tell me about yourself."

"Are you happy, Sylvia?"

"Yes, Neil, I am happily married." She emphasized the word 'married.' it was her way of drawing a line between them in the sand.

"What category does Mark fall into?" He quipped. He had not been impressed by Mark.

"The first," came the prompt reply.

"He surely isn't the macho motorbike man or exciting in any way," Neil remarked.

"I feel secure with him. He is not the kind of man women would fall head over heels in love with."

"You surely are in love with him."

"Yes," she was emphatic, to his displeasure.

"He is lucky. I envy him."

Where do you live now, Neil?"

"Oh, a few blocks away from my previous place. I gave Sonia all the properties and give her a considerable chunk of my paycheck, which keeps her satisfied. I have seen to it that my kids are well provided for, that they lack nothing, though I am left with nothing much at the end of the month. The kids are my solace, my joy, and they love me, and we get along well. I am restarting from scratch, though."

Sylvia wondered if it was the guilt or the fear of losing his children in an acerbic battle in the divorce courts that had made him give away all his wealth to his ex-wife and kids. "At least you could have kept one of the houses and some money for yourself instead of incurring these financial woes," she lamented.

"I am at peace with myself. My children love me. I may have lost them otherwise," he said matter-of-factly. "I did not want to put them through bitterness, and I wanted to make sure that they felt secure."

"I think you are in denial."

He had not seen this blunt side of Sylvia. For the most part, Sylvia's words tread on a tightrope of balance. She was the diplomatic kind who always hesitated to call a spade a spade. Over the years, people had found her endearing and a good listener. They would open up to her, not having to worry about being judged. She had felt this to be a weakness.

Then again, a spade could be interpreted by some as a weapon. So, who was she to call it a spade? People were different, each with a perspective of their own.

Prostitute

"I went to a prostitute last night," the words left Neil's burdened chest.

If Sylvia was aghast, she hid it. There was silence in the air, which Neil was desperate to break.

"Scold me, tell me I am a horrible person."

Sylvia looked away. He had fallen from the pedestal she had kept him on. Sylvia, who could quickly formulate words, was dumbfounded.

Anger seethed through her, finding it difficult to quell; moving away from him, she said, "just be careful you don't get STD's or STI's as they call it now."

He restrained a chuckle. "Is that all you can think about? Sylvia, I am sorry."

"Remember, we are not lovers anymore. We are just friends," she said, emphasizing the word 'friends.'

"Yes, yes," he agreed, exasperated. "We are just friends."

Sylvia was not sure if he was teasing her or actually meant what he said.

"I feel like a loser, a man incapable of seducing a real woman. I am so ashamed of myself."

She wondered if prostitutes were only breasts and buttocks and not real women.

"A man cannot be happy having sex with a woman as she pretends to respond and coo fancy words in his ears," Neil went on.

Sylvia was not keen on hearing the intricate details.

"It left me with a void, a hollow emptiness as if I had lost my virility—that I had to buy sex. I shudder at the thought."

"I am shuddering at the thought, too," was all Sylvia could come up with.

"Why did men reach out to prostitutes? Rich, powerful, and famous men did that too." Neil justified almost as if they were a different species. "They could get any woman they want! Women who want a ticket out of their meager living, women who wish to feel worthy associating with them, women who want an ego jolt when wanted by them. Sometimes women want a sugar daddy to take them places, lavish them with homes, expensive gifts, and even launch their careers."

"What about love and respect? Most women want that above anything else," Sylvia defended her species.

Neil was not listening; he was on a justifying spree, defending his own actions. "I think men went to prostitutes because they were tired of pursuing, seducing women or quite frankly tired of the dating scene, weary of rejection, bored of their wives or sex-starved."

"They were like the peacock languorously chasing the peahen," she disrupted his lengthy explanation to lighten the scene.

Colors on the horizon turned orange as the sun started to set, giving way to pink and mauve. In the midst of their intense conversations, they had been oblivious of the crowds of people who were now packing up and returning home.

"Let's go in and have some dinner." The sea breeze and the stroll on the beach had famished her. She needed a drink to swallow the bitter pill he had given her, to drown the bitter truth he had revealed to her.

They sat opposite each other, staring through the window of the restaurant. Dusk was settling in. People were walking along the cobblestone path, some entering the restaurant, some leaving. Luckily, the music was not blaring and drowning all noise— they were glad they could hear each other.

She noticed him staring at her. His eyes revealed no lasciviousness—they were forlorn and remorseful.

"I wish life were simple," he said dejectedly.

"Then it wouldn't be life, isn't it? It is as simple or as complex as we make it."

'Life was about conquering challenges, about overcoming them, about dreams and realizing them. And these dreams would chase us till our graves.' Mark had once said. She had hugged Mark for these words. The hug had gone into passionate lovemaking.

Neil was in awe of Sylvia's words, her simple explanations. He stretched his hand across the table to hold hers. She let him hold her hand.

Appreciation

Sylvia found Neil's eyes looking at her with veneration. She turned her gaze away from him and slowly wiggled her hand out of his grasp.

Later that night, she wrote:

Admiration was the greatest aphrodisiac for men and women. Love, sex, and money seemed secondary to the human need for approbation, yet it was the least talked about. It was free and yet least given. Genuine appreciation could cover flaws, accept flaws, could create wonders between people, friends, family, and colleagues.

Adoration is what creates an overwhelming sensation during the first flush of love. The alchemy of love is intangible yet made two people crave for each other. When the loving alchemy dissolves, we must try and bring it back to its imperfect but beautiful state. If unsuccessful, we could move on and go our separate ways. Maybe for a month or even a few months, we could wallow in self-pity, heartbroken, cry our hearts out, reel against the suffering imparted to us by the very person we had loved, given our soul and body, but then we have to garner our strength and create a new life for ourselves. We owe it to ourselves.

Our naivety, which had impressed the other now an annoyance. The powerful love which had initially adored our intricate expressions now abhorred by them. The love which had overlooked our oddities now found blemishes in everything, what was irresistible once, now a torment—our allure and seductiveness which was charming then, now a threat to the other's existence.

And if you find yourself in tears after three months of a breakup, pat your bruised ego, talk to it. For now, it is not about the jilted lover or the betrayal; it is about your bruised ego. Brush it off and move on. Men find it harder to heal the bruised ego. Women could cry it away, men bottle it inside them, and their ego is not just bruised but shattered. They brush it under the carpet, not even acknowledging the hurt to themselves, pretending it never happened, deceiving themselves. Men should learn to cry.

"We expect too much from ourselves, our loves," she told Mark over the phone that night.

"Stop watching those chick flicks and grinding your nose into romantic novels. They are not the reality," he said sagaciously. "How was your day?"

"Interesting," without going into the details. She did not mention her meeting with Neil. She rather spare Mark the agony of feeling threatened and herself a tirade of speculative queries. She decided to leave it at that.

Sometimes revealing too much of yourself can become a perilous thorn in a marriage.

Female Orgasm

Sylvia contemplated:

She surely could not reveal everything contrary to the cliché that 'married couples should have no secrets.' How could that be true when we could not even admit some of our thoughts to ourselves?

She surely did not want to know if Mark thought of that voluptuous actress when they made love.

Once Sylvia's friend Emma had revealed to her that she thought of her neighbor Johnny when getting an orgasm with her husband was difficult. Sylvia had smiled. They both had agreed that some things were better left unsaid. "Your husband won't find that very pleasant," Sylvia added.

Somehow a Johnny intervention helped to sort it out and reach that space of genital pleasure.

Sylvia continued her diary:

The genital pleasure was momentary, a struggle in one's mind to obtain it at any cost, to perform, to come with the partner, the timing usually causing a lot of strain and angst, sometimes due to the asynchrony, sometimes not climaxing at all but creating angst, all the same, to reach and revel in it.

Somehow it seemed easier for a man. An erection, usually culminating in an orgasmic climax pleasuring him acutely for a few seconds.

For a woman reaching a vaginal orgasm was like a ravaging war, the intense focus, getting blood into those vital organs, the momentary anxiety till one achieved the triumphant success.

Yes, orgasm was not as easy as the movies depicted, and many women rarely experience it. The familiar movie scene where the hero and his girlfriend plop on their soft pillows separated with exhilaration—the broad smile of smug satisfaction on their face as the Love God blesses them with pleasure made it all seem so easy, bereft of any complexity.

Love was different—it was a need for each other, the pecking, the necking, the niceties, the smiles, the eyes feeding off each other, the flowery words, and the flowing alchemy—the companionship cherished, the love all-encompassing. There was no space for a Johnny intervention or an imaginary intruder to cement the relationship.

Love and sex were intertwined yet distinct.

Human Emotions

Sylvia had read somewhere about love and wonderment. Every human emotion came with a price, she thought and continued writing:

> *When we know love*
> *We respond with wonderment.*

> *When we know appreciation*
> *We respond with deference.*

> *When we know trust*
> *We respond with faith.*

> *When we know kindness*
> *We respond with empathy.*

> *When we know censure*
> *We respond with skepticism.*

When we know indifference
We respond with bitterness.

When we know hate
We respond with vengeance.

She finished her diary and looked at the time. It was past midnight. Yawning, she kept her writings in the chest of drawers and went to sleep.

That night Sylvia dreamt that she and Miriam were at the Central Park in New York City, their hair all gray and their faces wrinkled, laughing away as they usually did when they met. Living in different cities, Sylvia had not met Miriam as frequently as she would have liked to.

Miriam had been diagnosed with an aggressive brain tumor. Sylvia wrote peppy letters to her in an attempt to keep her spirits up. But Miriam's condition was deteriorating. Sylvia prayed for Miriam, hoping that some miracle would cure her. Somewhere Sylvia knew in her heart that there was no hope, yet she did not want Miriam to lose hope. She did not wish to take hope away from Miriam.

Hope is what kept us, humans, alive, hope for better days, hope for better conditions, hope for better health, hope for more wealth, the hope of a brighter future.

176

Death

The phone rang. It was 3 am. Sylvia woke up, alarmed, apprehensive. Nobody called her at this time unless something was not right.

"Hello."

"Hello, hello, tell me," her voice impatient with foreboding.

"Miriam just died." The line went dead.

Miriam, her fun-loving, bubbly, talkative friend with a penchant for travel, had died. Sylvia plunked herself on the sofa staring at her past—a past in which Miriam had played a crucial part. She looked at the photos on her phone, gazing at the pictures of Miriam and her taken during their travels.

When they had gotten together, it was as if time had stood still. On a road trip to Door County, Wisconsin, Sylvia recalled how they were transformed into giggly teenage girls, teasing one another.

A few years ago, they had taken a trip to picturesque Maine—the fun, the camaraderie was woven into a beautiful memory, soon after which Miriam was diagnosed with a metastatic brain tumor. The chirpy chatterbox would no longer speak from the stroke it had caused till her death one and a half years later.

Emma, their friend, had joined them on the trip to Maine. They were the three musketeers, three teenage friends on a road trip twenty years later, and nothing seemed to have changed. The teasing, the squealing, the jokes, the romanticism all seemed to be trapped in a timeless zone.

As they walked along the coast, looking at the ancient lighthouse, Sylvia asked, "Does our mind ever change? Two decades later, I don't feel a day older."

Their friend Emma replied, "They say change is the only constant in life."

"Growing old seems justified when I am with you, my friends," Sylvia continued with a wink.

"Some friendships never need to be renewed. They just never fade," admitted Emma.

Miriam had been impatient with all these self-actualization discussions. She was ready for some fun and action.

"A prankster then and a prankster now," Sylvia remarked and resigned herself to follow Miriam's well-organized trip. Miriam was like the wind, willful and unstoppable when she had made up her mind. She guided them to the top of the mountains—it was spectacular.

Atop the mountains, the wind blowing at them, struggling to keep their clothes and hats in place for the pictures, they breathed the rare air together, looking at the blue sky and the deep blue sea below. "Even the most beautiful pictures don't do justice to God's canvas," Miriam said, her eyes closed, breathing deeply, taking in the air of the mountains as the cable car swung with the high rejoicing wind.

"We should do this every year," they promised each other.

A month later, Miriam had a stroke. A stroke of bad luck had turned the tables and overturned the promises they had made to each other.

Miriam's death had not come as a surprise, yet Sylvia cried her heart away. The tears rolling down her cheeks could not fill the vacuum she felt in her chest. Deep friendships exist, and Sylvia loved Miriam for Miriam's generosity, her kindness, for the laughter and sunshine she spread, and above all, her vulnerability and lack of vanity. Sylvia took out the poem she had written for Miriam a year ago and read it to herself.

Ode to Miriam.

She makes us laugh.
With her chats and talks.

She is fun and funny.
She walks into a room, and it feels sunny.

She is beautiful inside out.
She teases me a lot.
But I know she has no malice in her heart.

We were naughty in college together and then lost each other.
Till we met at Central Park when she became a mother.

Our friendship grew leaps and bounds.
She touched my heart with all her sounds.

She organizes our getaways where we laugh till we ache.
And have picnics by the lake.

Knowing her has made my life richer.
Being with her has made me happier.

I thank her for those moments of fun.
And look forward to many more to come.

The beautiful memory brought a smile to Sylvia's face. Wiping the tears, she re-saved the poem which she had never shown to Miriam, regret overwhelming her.

That night Sylvia wrote a eulogy for Miriam even as tears overflowed:

We were thick friends in college, and then we lost each other.

Years later, she re-entered my life, giggling her way into my heart forever.

When she left for a different city, I shed a tear.

She said she would be back every year.

Then she broke her promise.

The tumor was her nemesis.

She made everyone laugh.

Then she cried for a year and a half.

She loved to talk.

Then she could not talk or walk.

She was very sad and ill.

Leaving a void nobody can fill.

I regret those lost years.

We would have shared lots of laughter and a few tears.

Now she is gone.

We are left to pick up the pieces and move on.

She taught us life is short.

Don't waste it in strife and retort.

A BEAUTIFUL SOUL HAS FLOWN AWAY.

A few years ago, Miriam had written an essay for the school magazine on the occasion of her alma mater's 25th anniversary at the editor's behest. A friend of hers had died of breast cancer.

This friend had called her after school for their daily walks. At the age of sixteen, when most kids discussed clothes, shoes, boys, or the movies, they were more inclined towards philosophy and literature.

It was a far cry from today's self-obsessed selfie time, a time where the attention span is dwindling at a fast pace, where reading half a page is exhausting. Books had been her best friend.

One could get lost in books, travel along with the writer into the quiet recesses of the mind. The day people stopped reading, and its place was taken over by the quickly moving visual media, our society would lose out on the beauty of the language, imagination would be stunted, and we would lose the quiet space to the exploding graphics which were hitting our eyes, brains, and minds.

Sylvia, fatigued by the tears running down her cheeks, absentmindedly turned the pages of the school magazine, which Miriam had lent her. There was the essay that Miriam had so poignantly written on her friend's life and death.

Recollections and Reflections

School

It was 20 years ago when my father had moved to Mumbai. I had completed the 10th grade in Dubai as an average student, somewhat shy and self-conscious.

Twenty years have gone by; memories buried deep. In an effervescent world with changing responsibilities, rarely a thought entertained for the formative years of my life. With this beautiful reunion ages hence, memories like creatures buried in sheets of ice and snow have resurfaced fresh, defeating time itself. Some clear as crystal, others hazy like sunrays penetrating through a cloud.

As I sit to write reflecting on the days bygone, perhaps one of the most important years which would impact our lives for the remainder of our existence, I am struggling to sift through the various anecdotes, clearing the mist from my eyes with a blink, as if that will bring more clarity to understanding that 16-year-old schoolgirl in glasses and a thick-oiled braid. Since then, these traits have been discarded more like a declaration of independence from the parental regime than the need for aesthetic enhancement.

It was the summer of 2000 when my father decided to temporarily move us from Dubai to India. Change of any kind always comes with its set of challenges, heartaches, memories left behind, the fear of the unknown along with the exhilaration of treading through uncharted waters. Which emotion takes precedence depends on the individual.

I was shy, growing up in Dubai. Of course, my mother states that I was then a sort of a leader among my peers. A trait if I had then, I seem to have lost over the years and do not care for anymore.

A week had passed since leaving Dubai. I did not miss it at all. My mother, who had been attuned to many family lunches, gatherings, and gossip, suffered from separation angst for years, the ache waning as the years passed.

Summer was long; I still had no friends in this new land. I would see a few girls laughing and talking, but as much as I longed to be a part of that camaraderie, the concept of introducing myself to strangers had not occurred to me then. Twenty years later, I would have no compunction doing just that. A few weeks later, a very fair, thin girl came up to me, her thinness accentuating her long-crooked nose, something she had no reason to be bashful about, but it caused her subtle, fleeting moments of anguish. She was bolder and braver than me for sure. She stated that she was Nadira, very assertively. Little did I know then that this would be the beginning of a friendship that would last through the storm and calm, marriage and raising children, illness, and disease, to end only with the end of her journey. There were intervals of silence as she moved from our childhood residence to the house she shared with her husband and in-laws and as I left for the USA.

Our rendezvous was restricted to my annual vacations in India, those were not the days when emails or mobile phones were popular, and letters were infrequent.

Every time I met her, I was struck by the wisdom and weight she had gained over the years. I began to lean on her knowledge, especially during my transition.

A few years before her death, she had said, "I want to teach people; I want to teach them about life, all that I have learned."

I stared at her in my naivety, unable to comprehend then the depth and meaning of what she meant.

I moved to India again in 2012 ostensibly to acclimate my children to the Indian culture. A move that has enhanced their understanding of cultures lets them blend into the eastern and the western way of life, as a lime squeezed into water. A move they and I are grateful for but intrinsically and more selfishly to fulfill my own need. As a child, I had left the shores of India fascinated by the new worlds I had been introduced to. Life in Dubai seemed magical to me. India was only 3 hours away!

It was when we moved to the West—I felt the umbilical cord had, for the first time, been brutally severed. India became a fascinating fantasy. Little did I realize that I was fantasizing about my carefree childhood in India and that just as I had changed, India too had changed, ironically, at an even faster pace. As I was swinging between my dreams and a dream world, I was jolted back to reality.

It was the spring of 2017—I went to visit Nadira at the hospital a few times. We never discussed her condition. She did not want to. Conversations centered around my decision to start anew in the United States.

All Nadira said was, "I am a winner, and I will come out of this."

She believed in the power of the mind over matter. I did too.

But the cancer was relentless. It had eaten her bones, the pillar of the human body, even at the time of diagnosis. It would not be too long before it encroached upon her vital organs. The only area it failed and failed miserably was in its ability to penetrate her mind. She was resilient.

I hugged her as I hurried to the airport. She walked me to the door, wishing me good luck. I was not sure if I would see her again. I had my doubts. I tried my best to hide them behind a fake smile. She must have guessed.

"See you next year," she said as I was leaving. I did not look back and kept walking lest I unveil my fears and doubts. I was skeptical about the chemo she had received. It was too aggressive, according to the oncologists I had consulted. I hinted that to her, but she wanted to believe in the physician she had trusted her life with. I was not sure if the chemotherapy had expedited her death or the extensive invasion of her body by the intruder. Either way, she had been overpowered. I suppressed my doubts from surfacing again. It would not have mattered.

I was busy in my own world. Our correspondence was limited, making me miserably guilty. I rekindled our conversations, wrote a few peppy letters. She wrote back more to advise me about my situation, whether it was to my liking or not, always speaking her mind. I seemed to be the diplomatic one, pretending to accept whatever she said. Maybe in my own way, I wanted her to feel good.

Gradually her letters stopped. A sinking feeling enveloped me. I finally found the courage to call her. Her mother came on

185

the line. Teary-eyed, she said, in a motherly cajoling way, "Ask her to eat something. She needs strength." Nadira was not fighting her fate anymore. She was resigned. She could not read my letters, but she would request her mother to read them to her.

Her mother remarked, "You have been a great friend. She loves your letters. I am glad she has a friend in you."

I was not sure if I was deserving of that compliment. I did not feel I had done enough. Nadira had been there for me more than she would ever know.

And then she was gone, resting peacefully in the arms of her mother, the woman who had birthed her, raised her, complained about her, and like all mothers do, protected her. Nadira's father was in his late 60's. That was the last time I spoke to them, more because I was at a loss for words. Did they need consolation or understanding or just to be left alone? Would my presence create a sharper pain in their hearts, which was already grieving?

A year or so later, I met with her husband, 'Dravid.' She called him that, and I did too. I saw her son, who smiled at me and continued playing with his toys. I felt I saw in him a note of recognition. He knew me to be a friend of his mother's. I wondered what was going through his mind. He was too engrossed with play.

I remembered Nadira's words, "I am trying to push him away, but he just gets closer to me." She had prepared him for her death, which she herself had anticipated.

I have not met with them in years. Nadira was the pivot around which all these relationships revolved. The pivot was no more, somehow, somewhere the other relationships disintegrated.

As I write this, I am inclined to revisit a part of her. Her son must be in middle school now. I am hoping he would be just what she had envisioned him to be.

This would not be to rekindle the pain, for pain has a way of dissipating once accepted and with time, but more to tell him about the strength and resilience his mother had, the stories of our childhood, of her and me on the school bus discussing the 2002 Olympics. The only Olympic Games I have watched with so much vigor and earnestness to discuss the events enthusiastically the next day on our bus ride to school.

I am sure he will be eager to absorb them. Yes, I will meet with him. To tell him that we studied for our exams together, we would talk for hours, making our parents wonder what 'under the sun' we spoke day after day. Yes, we talked about everything under the sun.

Nadira was the girl with the second-highest GPA in the class, and I was the topper of the class. Nadira would study a few days before the exams, and I would study every day that year.

Being the topper, many of you have commented on that and asked me how that experience was.

I shall not be modest about that achievement in my life. It was not just a dream; it was a fervor, feverishly pursued. It was an achievement unabashedly relished. It was a journey that transformed a shy, unsure child into a more self-confident girl. Total self-assurance came only many years later, but the foundation was set at that tender age.

I remember the spring in my step as our school principal then enquired about me, and a teacher described something about me in a laudatory manner, and I overheard it. It did bring a smile to my lips; my feet did a dance movement, involuntarily. Yes, the adoration of the teachers and the acceptance received created a sense of security in me. Looking back, that year in school was an extremely happy one. Nadira, Emma, and our pranks, childish in nature, with malice towards none, organization of quizzes and debates, the encouragement received in abundance from all our teachers—yes indeed, all this and more was packed into that one year.

Learning was fun; it definitely was not a chore. I clearly remember the day the results were to be announced; I was in a frenzy of fear. I got up sweating, ill with nervousness, the suspense unbearable, the results of a dream, a zeal, exciting in itself, which had pushed me that whole year were to be released.

My mom scolded me, "So, what if you are not the topper, and what if you are? It is no big deal." She was my leveler. I clung to her, though angry at what she had said. Perhaps her intention was to decrease the blow in the event of disappointment.

I was a topper; people were congratulating me. To me, it was just a big relief. What my mother had said seemed right. It was no big deal. I smiled and accepted the congratulations gracefully. I sensed pride in my father's eyes. My mother was not affected. Somehow, I was not affected. The elation, if I felt, lasted maybe a few minutes.

Looking back, the sojourn towards getting the prized certificate was more exhilarating than the paper certificate itself. The certificate was just a piece of paper, and it felt just that. This is perhaps true of all achievements in life.

And though by no means do I wish to demean the accomplishment, it did bring in periods of joy, acceptance, and pure delight; it is also not a precursor of future success and definitely not the only one.

Education, schooling is a trip to be cherished, relished, and enjoyed. Luckily for all of us, we were in an alma mater where we had the freedom to be what we chose to be. To receive unsurpassed attention, our teachers relating to us in the way they did, taking our interests to heart, encouraging us all the way, reciprocating to our needs, imbibing in us strengths that still stay with us. Very few schools, teachers, and students can boast of the camaraderie we share.

Sylvia closed the yearbook, thinking of the day Miriam had informed her about the brain tumor. Miriam's impending death from cancer was churning her, pulverizing her to face the worst suffering life could inflict. An existence lived with a penchant for life, now staring at those broken dreams.

Talking and walking had become an extreme challenge for this once vivacious woman. She was losing faith in resurrection, in a miracle that would cross her over to her past self. Tears flowed through her; hope thwarted with every day of retrogression.

With one stroke of the wrath of God, life had changed for her. Fear clutched at her core. A few weeks later, the tears had dried up. She would be strong and fight this devil slowly encroaching upon her, without a whisper, she told herself, but the question remained, "Why me? I never smoked, never did drugs, have no family history of cancers. Very few people are diagnosed with this cancer every year, and I am one of those freaks."

Sylvia was convinced that stress was one of the reasons our genes mutate to cancer and various other diseases. Stress, anxiety, and chronic unhappiness could lower the body's immunity—infection, illness, and cancer cells could then spread and occupy the space, encroaching upon the healthy cells. Surely there were other causes of disease like the food we eat, the environment we live in, or the genes we are born with, and the list can go on.

Mortality

That night Sylvia wrote in her diary:

The brevity of life:

We lived our lives contemplating our future, falsely believing in our immortality yet fearing death, and when it struck us like lightning without warning, we were never really prepared to accept it, to embrace it. We fought it perhaps as someone had said to get that one chance to make life right.

She thought of her forty-year-old colleague Brian with whom she had animated discussions on world politics and financial upheavals during lunchtime at work, whose Greek God-like, tall, well-proportioned athletic body with a clean-shaven head had not given Sylvia any reason to suspect that he was soon to die of cancer, that his mental anguish was worse than the physical pain, that the smarting paroxysms kept him from taking the stairs. Even as the chemotherapy was failing him, belief in his imminent future never left his mind.

"I am saving my family paid time off for next year. If I take it now, the benefits would be less. I would like to travel next year. I haven't seen many places. Rome has always fascinated me, but my wife cannot get leave from her job, and she doesn't want me to travel alone." As he was formulating these words and trying to figure out a way to solve his wife's 'leave' issue, a sharp pain jabbed his back. He stooped a bit now, and a few days later, he started to limp from the pain in his brittle bones. He told Sylvia, "The pain has worsened. This disease drains your body and doesn't allow you to travel." He had accepted his fate.

The skin seems to cloak and cover the ravages that the organs were subjected to. The mind continued to think of the future. Were we humans fated to bear the brunt of our thoughts. Were we wired to worry about a future we did not know about and could never know about?

He did not live to see the next year. Within a month, his body had decimated so much that he could not work. He left behind his wife and an autistic kid.

Death had squashed his dreams, his life, his family, and his child. Death was cruel.

How was one to tell a dying person, embrace it, accept it, and all would be well?

'Embrace it, accept it so that you can be at peace with yourself.'

We are visitors on this Earth. The only surety in this ever-changing world is death.

In some cultures, death is celebrated.

Is it because the inevitable has occurred?

Is it because death has resulted in the release from human bondage, the strife of the mind, the wars within of guilt, envy, worry, the fatigue of the mind and body all laid to rest, or perhaps it is the path to eternal existence?

Even in death, there was hope.

The hope of eternity.

Ashes to ashes.

Dust to dust.

And yet the living fought wars within and outside of ourselves. Our need to be right, to control, to guard our insecurities, we trampled others in an attempt to usurp energy from others.

Collectively the minds warred, countries warred, creating misery in its wake with no panacea within sight.

One cannot cause pain and not be in pain.

Pain begets pain.

Sylvia dreamt of Utopia that night. 'A garden of colorful flowers, bees, and butterflies flitting under the warm sun. People were throwing away their guns and ammunition as they hugged, sang, danced in togetherness and love, for they knew they had one life to live, and the most important things in life were free to be enjoyed by all.'

As the early morning sunlight streamed through the window, its cool rays touched her face—she woke up, stretched—a smile lingered on her lips from the dream.

Mark was listening to the news. "There has been a mass shooting at a Las Vegas hotel. So far, 58 people have died, and 851 people injured."

"Why do you listen to the news so early in the morning?" she snapped, screaming to bury the sadness she felt almost as if it was his fault that the utopia of her dreams had been annihilated.

Purpose Of Life

Sylvia went about her day trying to comprehend human existence, trying to make sense of all the tragedies which happen in our world. That day it all seemed incomprehensible, insensible.

'Where was peace?' she questioned. 'What was the purpose of it all?'

The next day she decided to give a lecture on the Purpose of Life and Happiness, letting her mind wander into its realms and recesses to decipher from all that she had learned. "Life was the biggest school," Mark had once said with a philosophical twinge; his words never ceased to impress her.

In the quiet of the night as the birds flew back home and the crickets danced and sang in the night air, Sylvia wrote:

The Purpose of Life is to be at peace with oneself and one's station in life and to make a small positive difference in the world.

People said it was to find your passion' and pursue it to fruition; sure, one must and can do well only what one has an inclination and an aptitude for, but passions ebbed with time, changed with time, were cloaked in various garbs. The journey could rock one's core, and the peak once reached surely did not bring everlasting joy.

Pleasure is ephemeral, transient, and fleeting.

Most people were caught in circles trying to fulfill the responsibilities of feeding, clothing, and educating their progeny that they were left with very little time to chase their passions.

Then again, fulfilling these everyday responsibilities is the purpose of life.

The world talked about attaining 'Success.' The definition of success was our default inheritance entrenched and ingrained by societal norms. It conformed to millions of dollars, a handsome spouse, the sprawling mansions, the outrageously overpriced clothes, the sparkling diamonds, perhaps immeasurable fame, or contemptuous power over others.

Success defined by society is insatiable.

Success is equanimity and harmony.

Success is peace of mind.

The world had forgotten to let its progeny know this simple truth.

The world had forgotten to acknowledge this simple truth to itself.

Success did not lie in achieving fame, for fame is fickle and evanescent.

It did not lie in creating an empire, for in building an empire, you may need to destroy others and, many a time, your soul.

Even if the empire was created with the best of intentions, it does not bring with it the promised jubilation.

Many a time, the zenith once reached did not bring the happiness schemed, conceptualized, or envisaged.

Mark leaned over her shoulder to read her diary. "Perhaps it is in creating a masterpiece."

"Everybody cannot create a masterpiece. Does that mean they have no purpose in life, or does it mean that they have to spend their lives looking for something bigger than themselves, in discontent?"

"Contentment stagnates growth," she heard her inner skeptic say. "Isn't progress the culmination of man's quest forevermore?"

She recollected the Guru's words.

'A wanting person is an unhappy person.'

'Focused action, concentrated action without thinking of the fruits of our efforts is the only salvation in life.'

She had read the works of Swami Vivekananda at the ashram: Work, Worship, or Philosophy were the ways to achieve peace of mind.

The next day standing at the podium, her mind was going through the moments of happiness, disgruntlement, and every other emotion she had felt, analyzing them, weighing them, juxtaposing them with centuries of wisdom and the modern concepts. She heard herself say:

"Life is never stagnant, it is dynamic, and it is up to us to flow with the tide or against it. Every obstacle can lead to a better future if you look at it as a lesson, every setback an opportunity if we deem it so. How we react to situations governs our inner well-being—counting our blessings in the face of challenge, our redemption.

The battle is fought within us.

The Divine in you manifests when you conquer Greed, Anger, Lust, Hate, Jealousy, Ignorance, Fear, and Worry with Divinity, Grace, Forgiveness, Equanimity, and Serenity.

Otherwise, these devils will taunt you, haunt you and cause you to lose sleep.

Free yourself of these mental bondages; otherwise, they will propagate and consume you.

Brush off these cobwebs; otherwise, it gets harder to extricate yourself from these spiders.

'Understand that these spiderwebs don't spare the rich, the famous, the powerful, or even the most successful in our world. They leech on to anyone.

Truly successful people are those who have conquered and won over these conflicts of the mind."

We All Feel The Same Pain When Pinched

Sylvia remembered the temple, which was surrounded by gardens filled with flowers and shrubs. The bells, the chanting, the mantras, the incense were all charged with a certain calmness. Adjacent to the temple were farmlands fringed with rolling hills. The walk through the farm and the rolling hills had been awe-inspiring.

Quoting a centuries-old verse, the Guru had said:

'One is a relative, the other a stranger, say the small-minded.

The entire world is a family, says the magnanimous.'

'Be detached, be magnanimous.

Elevate your mind, enjoy the fruits of freedom.'

The scriptures of the past considered; 'A person who has attained the highest level of equanimity, with a detachment to the rewards of material possessions,' a successful person.

"A wanting man is an unhappy man. From desires stem conflicts, from conflicts arose sorrow." She reiterated the Guru's words.

"There was hardly any time to celebrate the fulfillment of one desire when a new one leashed itself with ferocity. And then it was a human struggle to squelch it, beat it, and obtain it.

The forever wanting heart and the forever thinking head were a contraindication to happiness by their very nature. If life was a gift which it indeed is as only a minuscule of the millions of sperm and ova get to create life, then we humans were wasting it away—with our own inner conflicts. Somewhere most of our pain was our own creation, our need to feel superior to the next person, our ego eating away our minds. Once the noise was subdued, the ego tamed and let go; freedom took its space, and perhaps the promise of everlasting joy could become a reality and not remain an illusion.

We are so occupied with our travails, our misgivings, our regrets, our disappointments, our rejections that we are unable to still our minds in quiet reflection, contemplate the meaning of our existence.

We complain to others, to ourselves—we take life too seriously, even when death stares us in the face."

The Beauty Of An Ordinary Life

The Bliss of Anonymity

Sylvia continued the lecture:

"You do not have to be the best in your field to attain bliss, you can aspire to be, but you can still be at *Peace in the Ordinariness*. Finding the treasure at the end of the tunnel did not bring with it everlasting happiness, especially if the journey was filled with despair. The treasure was slimy and could slither away as soon as it was obtained. Men chased this treasure overwhelmed with fatigue, disenchanted beyond resurrection, losing sight of life itself and the beauty which was there all the time.

To be all-pervading is an allegory, a delusion, a myth our ego leads us to believe. To keep reaching for that mythical insatiable carrot dangling in front is to lose your present, which is the most valuable gift. Little do we realize that the commonplace life is a boon. The quest for the extraordinary is the bane of our society. The pressure to live the exceptional life of glamour and wealth contributes to the increase in depression and suicides among adolescents and adults.

The vast oceans had borders. Everything had an end, but the ruminating mind. It goes on endlessly, raging a wrathful war, uprooting, devastating, destroying everything in its path, every little 'peace or contentment' which is trying to surface, quelling it, crushing it, beyond recognition.

There is a mantra to preserve our sanity,

'I am complete, whole, and secure.'

In our need to complete ourselves, we ridicule others.

We control by creating fear.

We allow ourselves to love but with caution.

We allow ourselves to have wealth without knowing how to give or learning how to give.

We allow ourselves to feel better by bragging and boasting, without stopping to think, how fortunate we are.

Despite all our achievements, there remains a gnawing sense of inadequacy. The truth is we are busy accumulating because we feel incomplete.

Each one of us is complete, whole. You are the doer; stand aside for a moment, and observe your thoughts. Awareness of your thoughts is the first step in taking charge of your happiness.

Observe the train of thoughts as they pass through the revolving doors of your mind. They are relentless in their pursuit of creating havoc and wreckage. The mind is the battlefield where evil and good, sanity and insanity exist, and try to subjugate the other.

Harness your thoughts, tame your mind so you can be free, one of the greatest scriptures had stated thousands of years ago. Nothing was more true or relevant even today. Perhaps the novice student could start by focusing on the breath. Deep breathing has a profound effect on the relaxation of consciousness and our mind, but that was only the beginning.

When a distressing thought crossed the mind, nip it in the bud, pluck it out; otherwise, like a snake, it can spread its fangs poisoning every pore, every cell of the body, and eat away at the core of the human soul.

The only way to salvation is to be on constant vigil, guarding the mind against disturbing thoughts.

I want to end by saying, bliss was beyond pleasure, beyond the reverberations and the vacillations of the thought. It was where the cosmic dance and the human spirit sing in synchrony.

Thank you!"

"With this, I open up the podium for any questions," she heard the moderator say.

The arc lights were directed towards the audience. Sylvia noted a show of hands.

Some were eager for more, some of the faces were blank, some skeptical.

"Let us start with the person on the last bench."

Q: "Contentment stagnates growth, innovation, progress, to rise above poverty, improve our circumstances, and be prosperous."

Sylvia paused for a moment, reminiscing scenes from the ashram, recollecting the scriptures and the books on philosophy she had read with deep interest. She thought of the people who had crossed her path and their problems. She had learned the most from them—they had been her foremost teachers. She then replied.

Ans: "We are not debasing the ego entirely. It is a motivator for all that you said, and if it is done to improve your station in life, it is fine. You are working for the betterment of yourself and your family. But if it comes as a result of an egotistical myth to obtain immeasurable greatness, it becomes torture, an unattainable illusion. Contentment, peace, and grace can make us more productive, for we now start from the place of being true to ourselves. Starting from an ego's need to be better than someone else drags you down, is counterproductive, and begins from a place where worry and stress predominate. Contentment is not stagnation. Stillness is not stagnation."

Q: "Why do some people succeed, and others fail?"

Ans: "We as a society, like never before, are so obsessed with success that everyone who is not a celebrity or a multi-millionaire is deemed a failure. We are taught to attain more and more to reach this definition of success."

"Again, the definition of a successful life varies. Understand too that we can only be a better version of ourselves. We cannot achieve what someone else has achieved, for our journey is different, our mind is different— our intelligence just as our emotional quotient is different. You must have heard of the age-old adage, 'What we sow, so we reap.' Life gives everyone what they give to it. If you give it bitterness, it will give you just that. You are in control of your destiny. You have to decide where or what you want to be. Someone had said, 'We have the power to overcome obstacles, but most of us lacked the mentality.' Some of us would grow stronger with adversity, some would succumb to it, and some would quit. Being successful is growing stronger with adversity."

Q: "What is the purpose of life?"

Ans: Sylvia smiled. "The Guru has said—harmony with nature, with people, with the work at hand, with time and to be at peace with where you are at every moment is the purpose of life—accepting the present."

Q: "Does that mean you don't think about the future?"

Ans: "Worrying and obsessing about the future is different from setting goals and achieving them. The past is don—learn from it. The future is unknown, so stop the affliction of worry. The only tangible present given to you is this moment to make peace with it. Life is a consequence of the choices we make. If happiness is a choice, then unhappiness too is a consequence of our choice, our beliefs, our thoughts. Believe that you are in the place you are meant to be at this time because this is the place you worked for. You are the creator of your happiness and destiny.

We have the power to steer our life to the place we want. To bring that change, we have to shift our paradigm. But again, we can only be the best version of ourselves. Each of us is unique, and we cannot and should not want to live someone else's life.

Our purpose in life then is to understand the oneness of humanity and its differences and salute both so that we are at peace with ourselves and others."

There was silence.

"Nobody has asked me what the biggest failure in life is?"

The crowd perked up.

She continued, "The biggest failure is not having peace of mind."

After a moment, she added. "Now tell me, most people you know or look up to perhaps have money and mansions, but how many have peace of mind?"

This time there was thunderous applause.

Sylvia saw Mark walking towards her, smiling, speechless. He held her hand and led her away from the podium, his eyes wet with joy.

Epilogue

Seema And Neil

Seema did not remarry. She focused her energy on establishing a career; she was lonely many a day, but over the years, that became her norm, her life. She got used to her loneliness and independence.

Seema, who had always lived a sheltered life, first protected by her father, then under the shadow of her husband, became this fiercely independent woman, a leader of sorts in her community, an advocate for abused women.

She did not want it any other way. The trauma of her past had numbed with time. But men remained scary creatures, not to be trusted.

"I don't believe in happily ever after," she once told Sylvia. "That happens only with Cinderella."

Sylvia had smiled, not wanting to be disagreeable. She believed in 'happily ever after and the magic of love.'

Sylvia thought of getting Seema and Neil together. They both had been important pivots in her life.

'No, that would be painful for me. I would be very jealous if my ex and my very good friend got together as a couple,' she thought.

Sylvia took pains to see that their paths never crossed.

We are human, and sometimes the emotions of envy and jealousy loom large at us against our better intelligence. Even the most evolved of us could succumb to these emotions.

'I am a work in progress,' Sylvia wrote that night feeling guilty.

As for Neil, he dated a few women, none living up to his love for Sylvia, none reaching the pedestal he had kept Sylvia on.

Sylvia remained his confidante, his best friend—a sounding board when he had issues of any kind. He sought her advice when he had problems with his boss or girlfriends, and even his children until one day he decided to get married.

He arranged for his fiancée to meet Sylvia and Mark at a restaurant. Over the years, he had grown to like Mark. They both meant a lot to him.

"Sylvia is a good friend of mine," he said as he introduced Sylvia to his wife-to-be.

His fiancée sat throughout the meal, fidgety, observing them. She felt like an outsider, unable to fit into their society or partake in their conversations.

Later that night, she forbade Neil any further contact with Sylvia.

He had to make a choice. 'Marriage or friendship.'

He was desperate to be married.

That was the end of Neil and Sylvia's friendship.

Sylvia continued her work at the university and pursued a career in writing. She continued her quest to understand human nature, the intermingling of the physical and the spiritual, for each needed the other to lead a successful and fulfilled life. Mark supported her in her ventures. She loved his soul with all its imperfections.

The cord of love connected them and pulled them together.

Looking at Mark as he slept, she wrote:

'Behind every successful woman, there is a supportive man.'

Tame The Mind
Before It Is Too Late!

Please rate and review this book on the site you bought it, on Goodreads and Amazon.

Thank you for being a part of this journey with me.

https://tamethemind.org
tamethemind360@gmail.com

"**Enjoying this book** in serene and peaceful surroundings. Tame The Mind An Exploration of Love, Sex, Happiness.

Great piece of work, Dr. Asha Menon. ⚫⚫⚫⚫⚫⚫⚫ ⚫⚫⚫

Truly one proud moment for you.

Really like the manner in which all happenings in life were linked up in a simplistic way - school/ childhood, love, sex, friendship, marriage, work and family, success, freedom, dependency, insecurity, courage, and confidence. The poems are exemplary

A must-read for all ages, both to understand one perspective about life, as well as relate and reflect on what has already gone by. Gives a very **positive vibe** overall.

Suggest just pick it up and have a quick read - am sure you will enjoy it." Ms. Chopra.

Daring topics, masterful language, and delicate narration. This is an excellent piece of work.

Dr. Asha Menon has demonstrated her capacity to explore the circumstances and to present the mental state and abnormal situations people are put in or rather forced to face. More impressive is her ability to walk the fine line describing the close and intimate personal encounters, a line that can easily be crossed by an average writer.

Kudos to Dr. Menon for the daring selection of topics in her book that many in society would rather avoid. Most of us are hiding behind thick and wide facades, everything smelling like roses especially in this era of social networks. **Drawing upon her own rich experience as a physician, the author exposes the real human beings behind the facades as she explores the turbulence that each of the vulnerable characters is experiencing** and how that impacts their personal lives. The book gets into the details of the thought process as the characters drift through life, and how those underlying thoughts shape their personal and sexual relationships as well as love. Through the character of Sylvia quoting the 'greatest scriptures', the author then concludes that harnessing our thoughts and taming our mind is the best way for ourselves to experience the peace of mind and

thus the happiness we all crave. Bala Andhrapall

210